MW01241478

Hollows Grove

A Holinight Novella

Lee Jacquot

A HOLINIGHT NOVELLA

HOLLOWS GROVE

LEE JACQUOT

Cover Design: Cat at TRCdesignsbycat

A Quick Note From the Author

Hollows Grove is a standalone novella in the Holinights series. None of these books need to be read in order.

It is a steamy & fun read (seriously, it's just a good time) intended for mature audiences of legal adulthood age. It should NOT be used as a guide for kinks or a BDSM relationship.

The author is not liable for any attachments formed to the MCs nor the sudden desire to have someone make you come more than you think you can handle.

Reader discretion is advised.

To my readers looking for a good time, and a sexy twist on the best murder mystery game out there.

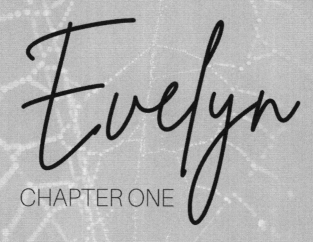

Evelyn

CHAPTER ONE

How is it that best friends always find a way to rope you into shit that makes you question your sanity? That makes you contemplate how in the hell you've stayed friends for so long?

Ciara knows I'm scared of *literally* everything. She knows I don't do spiders bigger than my thumb, I can't look at a clown without almost shitting my pants, and the last time I saw a scary movie, I was thirteen. And I only watched it because I was tricked under the pretense that it was a parody.

These are never-changing facts that she's been privy to since we met in fifth grade. Yet, here I am, putting the finishing touches on my Halloween outfit for her murder mystery party.

One that I'm not only helping *host* but am also *participating* in.

One where I could be the victim.

Or even worse, *chased*. I could end up like all those clumsy, token characters in the movies and fall down a flight of stairs or run smack-dab into a tree. So many potential catastrophes, and all of which have my name on them.

The only pro in the extremely long list of cons is that she's having me play the role of the maid. I consider it the singular

1

upside because if I'm going to be forced to run through a mansion and possibly fake murdered, I might as well look sexy as fuck doing it. Plus, there's always the off chance I get lucky and am paired with one of her hot coworkers, where we do less clue hunting and more body searches.

I check the tulle under my skirt one last time, making sure it's secure. I wanted to add a little oomph to my store-bought *hot maid uniform* and had to sew an extra layer of the itchy material into the waistband. But even knowing how incredible my legs will look in the outfit, my internal dread about the night doesn't ebb in the slightest.

I push out a heavy sigh. "I still can't believe you convinced me that this is a good idea. How the hell do I always let you talk me into stuff?"

My best friend turns, pushing one of her passion twists from her shoulder, and smirks. Her deep mauve lipstick is perfect for her role as *Lady Lavender* and pairs well with her pastel purple blouse. "Because in the almost twenty years we've known each other, there's nothing we won't do for one another."

I shake my head, twirling a loose string hanging from the bodice around my index finger and snap it off. "Yeah, but it's never involved being hunted down and murdered."

Normally, when I'm pulled into one of Ciara's shenanigans, it involves a random trip to an island, deep diving into her latest fling's social media, or staying up until four in the morning watching movies so she isn't lonely while she's doing her hair.

It's because of those same antics that I'm able to say I've seen a good portion of the world, made it through a seven-year relationship that ended in a failed engagement, and live in a spider-free townhouse. You know, because she's my own personal eight-legged arachnid eradicator.

"You won't be hunted down." Ciara lets out an exasperated sigh as she flips through the manila envelopes on the kitchen island for the third time. "And I'm doing this because, with my new position at work, I really need to do some team building with the staff."

"Yeah, and I have to go, why?"

She huffs. "Because you're my girl, and I need you there in case it doesn't go perfectly."

My eyes roll so hard that a sharp ache radiates through the back of them. "Since when does anything you do *not* turn out perfectly?"

She blinks for a moment, looking as though she might actually be able to recall a time when she *didn't* obsess over every minute detail of something until it was flawless. Then, of course, when the inevitable happens and she comes back blank, she laughs. "You're being dramatic, Eve. The mansion is used for more than just Halloween events. Really, it's not even creepy."

My mouth gapes open as I slap a hand on the counter. The sharp noise echoes off the walls, and the pain shooting up my forearm makes me acutely aware of how hard granite is. "My ass! I saw the photos. They go all out for Halloween. That's not even *including* the surrounding woods and the cliff it's next to. At night, that place is the epitome of terrifying, Ciara."

"It's a wedding venue," she says a little too wearily as she slips the envelopes inside a large bag. "I don't get why you're still so sca—"

"Because of *your* brother," I hiss the obvious before she can finish. "And wedding venue? The only people getting married in that house on the hill are *The Addams Family* fanatics and ghost hunters."

"Again, you're being dramatic."

I hop down from the barstool I've been warming for half an

hour and scoff as I stretch, "About which part? Your brother or the estate? Because I have irrefutable facts, some of which are decades old, as to how I'm not."

She narrows her eyes, but she knows she doesn't have a good rebuttal because the estate is so horrifying at night, it's been used in horror movies. Two of which were slashers where victims did, in fact, get run off the cliff.

She's also well aware that her brother is an asshole. At least, he is to me. Has been since I moved here when I was ten. It was shortly after my father decided staying together as a family wasn't worth it anymore, and split.

Most small-town people know that remaining there following a failed marriage is shit, which is why my mom and I moved to a new city in hopes of a fresh start.

Ciara and her family happened to be our next-door neighbors, and it didn't take more than a week of walking home from school together before I was at her house every day.

Soon after, the Davis family became part of mine. Mrs. Davis always sent me home with dinner, and since my mom was a nurse and didn't get home till almost eight, it was always a nice treat. On the weekends, Mr. Davis would help my mom with any issues around the house. Ciara's parents gave her the break she needed and peace of mind knowing I was cared for when she was at work.

Everything was perfect. It made the ache of missing my parents together seem almost nonexistent, and there was never a time when I longed for life before the divorce.

And it was all thanks to the Davis family. Well, three out of the four. Ciara's older brother was a complete dick. The worst person imaginable. The splinter I could never get out.

He's three years older than Ciara and I, and man-oh-man, I wanted to deck him in the face on more than a dozen occasions.

At first glance, he's fucking hot. Like unbearably beautiful, with a smile that should be in every toothpaste commercial, and the personality of a humble jock who is just as smart as he is talented. If you asked anyone about him, they'd say he's the sweetest young man they've ever met, and how he wouldn't hesitate to give a stranger the shirt off his back.

But if you asked me? I'd say the complete opposite because, for some reason I still don't understand, he's got a fascination with scaring me.

It started with him putting fake bugs in my food and hiding around dark corners when I would stay the night. He did any and everything he could to get me to lose my shit.

When I asked him why, he said he enjoyed making me scream. He got the biggest kick out of it, and no matter how mad I got, it only made him want to do it more. Or do something worse.

One time, he stood over me when I was sleeping and just stared at me until I woke up and saw him hovering over me. After that, I don't think I got a good night's sleep until he left for college.

Hell, even then, I always double-checked doors and triple-checked under my bed.

I won't lie, though. There were times—albeit brief and fleeting—when I saw the guy everyone talked about. The sweetheart under the mask. There was even a time I entertained the thought of seeing in what other ways he could make me scream, but the idea vanished quicker than it came.

Now, even knocking on thirty, he still fucks with me, which is why I actively try to avoid him. Which leads me to my current dilemma; we're helping Ciara host the event.

Together.

Yes. Not only do I have to endure an evening full of what

5

goes bump in the night, but I'm doing it with the man who is the literal cause of my fear of the dark.

I glance back at Ciara, waiting for her to try and tell me I'm exaggerating about her brother or the estate.

After another moment, she purses her lips and moves them back and forth, the challenge to prove me wrong evident in her bright brown irises. But we both know the truth, and she rolls her eyes in defeat.

"Exactly," I chide, opening the refrigerator and taking out one of the Canadian sparkling waters. I swear these things have some type of addictive additive in them. "So now I have to ask, what did I do to deserve this punishment you're subjecting me to?"

"He's gonna know you took one." Ciara points, cleaning the rest of the papers off the island and ignoring my question.

"And? I think it's safe to say he owes me a few." I hold the drink up in a faux toast, only to immediately have it swiped away.

"Hey!" I whirl around, and I let out something that's supposed to resemble a gasp but ends up turning into a distorted snort when I see who it is.

Ciara's brother, Dorian—the bane of my existence, the gray hair standing out in my sea of brown waves, the itch I can't reach—stands two feet away from me and tips my water against his annoyingly perfect lips with a wink.

He's dressed in black joggers and a plain white shirt, yet the fit looks tailor-made, molding to a broad chest and narrow waist that meets muscular thighs. I swear his picture should be hanging outside of an athletic store window.

Dorian's dark eyes seem to shimmer under the kitchen light as he takes another heavy gulp before nodding toward me. "Thanks, E. I was parched."

"That was mine, you ass." I narrow my gaze, contemplating

whether or not I should snatch it back. But he's had his mouth on it, and knowing him, he'll turn it into some kind of innuendo that just stirs up more shit. Aside from scaring me, he loves making me squirm because he knows I somehow still find him attractive.

It was probably that time I saw him save a cat from a tree outside his house. I mean, who actually does that? In his prom tux, no less. Or it could have been from the Halloween party five years ago. The one I'm still trying to forget to this day...

Yeah. It was probably then.

"Funny. I don't remember you asking me if you could have one." He takes yet another sip, and I curse my traitorous eyes from watching his throat roll with the action.

Of course, he catches me, and the light brown skin at the corner of his eyes wrinkles as he grants me a lopsided smirk.

I ignore the way my stomach does some unwarranted jerk that could easily be mistaken for gas and spin around, grabbing another bottle from the fridge. "I don't have to ask. Half the time, I'm the one who buys them when I go grocery shopping with your sister."

Dorian and Ciara live together in a townhouse four units down from me, so I'm over more often than I'm not. Luckily, Dorian is usually out of town scouting potential recruits for the university he coaches football for, so we rarely cross paths.

"Well, sunshine, you didn't buy these." He starts to reach for my glass, but the look on my face gives him pause. After a second, he relents and shrugs. "I spit in all of them anyway. Enjoy."

My fingers tense around the top before I twist it off. When it doesn't crack from the safety seal separating, my internal debate over what I should do begins.

He's trying to call my bluff—something he does regularly—

and scare me into bowing out. I don't particularly believe him, but I also don't really want to chug his saliva either.

Another moment passes, and I consider just letting him win this one, but the smug look on his face is reason enough not to care. I tip the glass back and take a heavy swig. The bubbles burn my throat on the way down, and the minute drop in his smirk is enough to make swallowing whatever might be in the bottle worth it.

Naturally, my triumph is short-lived.

"You like my spit in your mouth, sunshine?"

I almost choke on the water as Ciara makes a gagging sound that's a little too realistic. Slamming the glass on the island, I shoot him the bird. "Fuck off, Dorian."

He shrugs again, finishing his drink that's meant to be savored, and looks at his sister. "You regret this decision yet?"

"I did the moment I asked." Ciara sighs, tossing her bag over her shoulder as she shakes her head. "We leave in twenty, y'all, and for the love of God, please, *please*, be nice tonight. It's only like six hours of your entire life."

I throw a hand out. "It's him you need to be talking to."

Ciara is already halfway to the front door, but she stops to give me a look that says the words before she does. "You're just as petty, Eve. Do I need to remind you of the time you put cayenne pepper in his underwear?"

"Ciara!" I whirl around to see Dorian's mouth wide open.

I'd never admitted I did it, and in the end, he had to make a doctor's appointment because he thought he'd caught something from one of his hookups. I felt bad, but not bad enough to confess and face his wrath.

Dorian doesn't say anything for at least ten awkward seconds as his eyes flit between me and her, before clamping his mouth shut. He nods more to himself than to us and grabs his keys off the counter, brushing past me without another glance.

"Y'all meet me in the car when you're ready."

I exchange a look with my best friend, whose mouthed 'sorry' does nothing to ease the flurry of anxiety testing out my heart muscle's dexterity.

Well, shit.

Evelyn

CHAPTER TWO

T o say the ride to Hollows Grove Estate is one of excitement is a complete and utter lie.

The atmosphere is thick, almost unbearably so, as Dorian drives us to the mansion. Every once in a while, the steering wheel creaks with the pressure of his grip, and he keeps going an abnormal amount of time without blinking, making it clear what he's doing.

Dorian Davis is planning my murder.

It's probably hypothetical, of course, but it's coming, that much is obvious, and now my fear about the evening's event has escalated to astronomical heights.

See, I talk a big game, but Dorian knows how to pull emotions out of me no one else can. He knows which fears cause the loudest screams and the most visceral reactions. The notion he's going to play on every single one of them tonight has my palms slick, my stomach in knots, and my throat painfully dry.

Five Years Ago

"How did I let you talk me into this?" I tug on the edge of my pleather shorts that feel as though they're painted on my skin. They don't budge.

Ciara gestures to said shorts and then up the broad cement steps of her sorority house. "Because one, you look hot. Two, you needed to get out and get your mind off that boyfriend of yours—"

"Ex," I correct her, my eyes doing a quick survey over the many variations of sexy professions as they enter the party.

Ciara scoffs. "Yeah, well, I doubt this is permanent, considering you've been together since high school. Plus, you know you love your safety net."

Ouch. I want to roll my eyes or maybe even shrug her off, but she's not wrong.

Brad and I have been seeing each other since our senior year, and he is what she says—safe.

He plans to join his father in engineering, which alludes to security. He wants a picket fence around a quaint house in the suburbs, meaning stability. And he gives me an orgasm almost every other time we have sex, which I'd say is pretty decent, so there's that.

I think it's also important to note we get along, which is a huge plus, considering I'm sort of... opinionated at times.

Still, the closer we get to cementing our relationship with a ring, the more I worry if *safe* is what I want. After all, that's what my mom thought she had.

"Are we going in, or are you gonna let this little demon costume go to waste?" Ciara lifts an arched brow, but I don't think she realizes how much her cat whiskers take away from her intimidation tactics.

Still, I relent, pushing out a sigh that instantly causes her to perk up. "Fine. But the first green and red sweater I see, I'm out."

"Okay, okay. Promise."

"And for your information, I'm a succubus," I inform her as I follow behind.

She smirks. "Even better."

"I have to pee." I lean into Ciara's shoulder, hoping she hears me over the deafening roar of the party.

The DJ has been blaring Halloween songs at full blast, and my only guess as to why the place hasn't received a noise complaint yet is because all the neighbors who could possibly complain are here.

The sorority house is filled to the brim with the undead, the sexy, the disgusting, and people that clearly need a job in Hollywood doing special effects makeup. With the added orange glow from the pumpkin string lights and smog machine that goes off every few minutes with the flashing orbs, I'd say I'm doing fairly well mentally. I think I've only jumped once, and it was because when a wolverine bent down to tie their shoe, its large nose brushed against my skin. I hadn't expected it to be *wet*.

Ciara stops dancing and nods, pointing to the stairs, where a group of zombified jocks chug a keg through a clear hose. "Go up to my room."

"Oh, you're magical. Thank you."

Quickly, I weave through the crowd, somehow able to make it to the base of the steps without running into anyone too... clowny.

Upstairs, it almost feels as though I'm in a different house. The music is muted, muffled behind the closed door of Ciara's room. It's quiet enough that my eyes linger on her bed longer than necessary, wondering if I could get in a nap unnoticed.

A twinge in my bladder prompts me otherwise, forcing my

feet to her en suite bathroom. After I'm done, I wash my hands and the spot on my arm that is still gleaming with whatever residue the guy put on the end of his nose.

As I slip the hand towel from the bar, a weird tingle shoots across the back of my neck, causing the fine hairs there to stand at attention. Without looking up, I can almost guarantee someone is behind me, but fear cements my feet in place, rendering my limbs damn near useless. My throat squeezes tight, dread working through my core as my hands stop the motion of drying.

Where's the adrenaline? Isn't that a thing? Shouldn't my heart be pounding so hard that I have quicker reflexes?

Fight or flight?

Something?

The concept must only be true in the movies because my arms drop to my sides as if they weigh two tons each, and my eyes drag way too slowly up my frame in the mirror to the figure behind me.

He's tall, about a foot taller than me, and built with lean, defined muscles, evident in the window of his open black button-up. The smooth dips and ridges of his chest are familiar to me, having seen them on display on more than a few occasions, but my body's visceral reaction is not.

Maybe it's because my breath has become shallow, the lack of air suffocating as I take in the reflective silver mask covering Dorian's face, but the strange tingle from my neck sinks down through my core, causing my thighs to squeeze together. Because he's been stored away, studying for his finals for his master's degree, I guess I hadn't thought he'd be here. Now, I feel dumb for not knowing better.

Dorian remains perfectly still, his dark eyes roving over the small bits of fabric covering my frame. Everywhere his eyes touch, he leaves a trail of heat that melts into my skin and has me suddenly unbearably hot.

His head tilts slightly. "That boyfriend of yours let you wander off all alone?"

Thankfully, the comment gives me enough spark to find my voice. "Ex. And I'm not a dog on a leash."

I can almost swear a glimmer passes through his eyes, but with the distance, I can't be sure. "I didn't say you were. Though I think you might be sexy in a muzzle."

A flare of anger and arousal blooms in my gut. That should *not* turn me on in the slightest, but the way his voice dropped and the hungry look in his eyes...well, it kinda does. Still, I bite back. "And I wonder if I threw a stick if you'd go fetch it."

He takes a step forward, and I stiffen, my nerves drawing tight. "That depends. Since when aren't you and the tool dating?"

One of my shoulders hitches up. It comes off as nonchalance, but really, it's the only thing my muscles are capable of. "A couple weeks."

Another step. "Why?"

"I don't know—"

"You don't know why you broke up with a guy you've been with for four years?"

Since when did it get so hot? My skin is fucking burning, and the pleather outfit doesn't make it any better.

My lips thin, a hand finding my hip. "I don't know *why* you think it's any of your business."

His silver mask lifts slightly, and I imagine him smiling beneath it. I've always liked that damn smile. "You are my business, sunshine."

My brows snap together, agitation flushing through me. There's been a few times I've overheard him referring to me as "just another little sister," and it infuriates me. Why? Maybe because it made the attraction I had toward him feel weird, or perhaps it was the way I knew he viewed me as nothing more than something to take care of. Either way, I hated the insinuations.

Finally, I will my body to whirl around, a retort tickling the edge of my tongue, but when I do, Dorian has eaten up the remaining distance between us and is one big breath away from our chests touching.

I suck in a sharp breath, the close proximity and his deep aroma doing a number on my libido, while the fear from seeing him in the intimidating mask fades into an odd arousal.

"I wonder..." He leans down, his eyes lowering to my throat, before gliding back up. He reaches a hand behind him and flips off the bathroom light, plunging us into complete darkness.

Panic sweeps over me, my heart slamming into my chest as I grab onto the front of his shirt.

He chuckles, the rough side of his index finger hooking under my chin. I can't see him, but I can *feel* him, his warm breath coasting over my mouth and sprouting goosebumps down my arm.

"Tell me, E. Are you scared?" He leans in, the cool feel of the plastic running along my jaw making me shiver. "Or wet?"

I don't get to answer.

"EVE!" Five loud bangs ring out against the bedroom door, making me nearly jump out of my skin.

Dorian chuckles, dropping his hand, flipping on the light, and stepping backward just as Ciara flings her door wide open. She steps in, pushing past her brother as if he wasn't two inches away from my face thirty seconds ago, and snatches my hand. "They're playing my song. I need a partner, and none of my Soros knows how to do it right."

Present

My leg bounces violently as I recall the Halloween party.

Up until that moment, the undercurrent between him and I was just that—an implication. Nothing too forward or obvious. But Dorian changed something between us that night. Crossed a line we unknowingly drew the day we met.

He also brought a fantasy I didn't even know I had to the surface, and it was damn near clawing at my chest to get out.

When I tried to find him later, though, the flock of females he was entertaining reminded me why I always went back to the safer option of my ex.

I didn't think I'd regret getting back with Brad and letting Dorian be a missed opportunity. But when Brad got down on one knee a few months ago, and I saw brown eyes instead of his bright blue, I knew I couldn't do it.

It wasn't because I actually wanted to marry anyone else, but because I didn't want to marry him, and that wasn't fair to either of us. I couldn't relive what my parents went through.

I want someone I can have fun with. Someone I can argue with freely without worrying I'll hurt their feelings. I want to be pushed to my limits, not encouraged to be content with complacency.

I want the type of love that makes my heart feel like it's going to leave bruises on my ribcage from beating so hard.

A familiar tingle radiates across the back of my neck, and I know without looking that Dorian's eyes are on me.

Evelyn

CHAPTER THREE

"Alright, we're a little early, so we have plenty of time to set up." Ciara stretches out like a cat, arching her back and straightening her legs as far as she can while Dorian pulls onto a private road lined with trees.

It only took half an hour to get here, but in just that short time, it seems as though we've driven into a completely different state.

The sun is still fairly high, illuminating the autumn hues creeping onto the leaves. The lawn visible through the trees has been recently manicured, the bright blades of grass standing at an even height, as though someone cut it with a leveler and a pair of scissors. The long driveway is prettier than the pictures depicted, and the loose-looking gravel feels like smooth concrete under our wheels.

The estate comes into view as he takes a slight curve up the incline, and if I wasn't already insanely nervous about the night's events, I might be able to appreciate the beauty even more than I surprisingly already do.

It's a two-story mansion with a face of bleached bricks so white they almost look like slates of marble. Black window frames match the massive iron doors, and the pops of color from pumpkins resting on the front steps add the perfect accent.

Seeing it in person, not adorned with Halloween decorations seen in horror movies, does make my pulse ease slightly. Even the hedges next to the estate appear more romantic now, and I'm able to imagine some bride walking through them to her husband, who's waiting at the edge of the beautiful cliff to sail into forever.

But then, of course, Dorian pops my bubble. "Can you imagine being chased through there? So worried about looking back, you slip over the edge and plummet to your death?"

Why do I even bother trying to be positive?

I cut my gaze to the rear-view mirror and catch his gaze already locked on me. Suddenly, I wonder if the comment was less of an observation, and more of an ominous threat. The corner of his eye crinkles as he smiles and shoots me a wink.

My stomach does an involuntary clench, but I mask it with an eye roll. "Imagine doing the chasing and being so dense, you fall instead."

He releases a low grumble of a chuckle that only makes the tightness in my core worse, and I groan my annoyance. I fucking loathe the way no matter how much I can't stand him, I still *really* like that sound. It makes me hate him more.

I break the short-lived staring contest and peer out the window. "Make sure after we set up, you keep your distance. I don't have time to entertain your theatrics tonight."

Ciara clears her throat as we pull in front of the entrance. "About that..."

My face snaps to glare holes in the back of her head, and as if she can actually feel the burn, her shoulders slump. "You'll be paired up tonight during the game."

Before I can register exactly what she said or even try to clarify, she jerks the door handle open and nearly jumps out of the car, the murmured confession leaving a trail of fire behind her.

Dorian sighs, seemingly unbothered, almost as if he knew it was coming, while my heart has taken up residence in my esophagus. "Did you know she was going to do that?"

He shrugs nonchalantly. "I mean, it's not a surprise considering we're *dressed* as a pair."

The maid and the butler.

"So?" I bite, annoyed with myself I didn't catch that not-so-subtle detail before. "The maid wasn't paired with the butler in the movie."

He places a big hand on his own door handle. "Yeah, well, we're also helping her host the event, E."

Irritation slithers up my spine. It leaves a nasty feeling too close to trepidation clinging to the bone. If I thought looking over my shoulder all night was less than ideal, having the trouble right next to me is even worse.

I pinch the bridge of my nose while letting a defeated sigh pass my lips. "Can we pause this little game of yours tonight? Just this once, please?"

He doesn't even hesitate. "No."

"Dammit, Dorian. Why?"

"Because it's my favorite game to play." His voice is smooth, coated in something I can't quite place, as though it's the easiest question he's ever been asked.

With a lopsided grin, he exits the car, leaving me with an emotion I don't let myself acknowledge. What I do wonder, though, is if tonight's party will be like the last one we went to all those years ago.

If things will come to a head and we'll finally put an end to the back and forth once and for all.

After a few minutes of considering what tonight will be

like, I begrudgingly get out of the car, storm up the massive steps, and into the mansion.

Unlike the outside, the interior is *exactly* what the pictures online showcased.

At first glance, it's beautiful. Stark white walls, an overbearing chandelier hanging low between two sets of stairs on either side of the foyer. Straight ahead is a fireplace surrounded by dark stones resting beneath a long, thick wood mantle. The marble floors and pristine furniture fit with the modernness of the place, and for a moment, I can see why people spend a pretty penny to use this place as a wedding venue.

But then, in the blink of an eye, horror—or, more accurately, the long strings of fake spider webs Ciara draws out of her bag—corrodes the beautiful image. In an hour's time, this house will look like Morticia Addams's getaway villa.

As if on cue, Ciara nods behind me to her brother, who's dumping the rest of the bags from the trunk at the front door. "The owners said there's a ladder in the back, Dorian. It'll help you reach those bars running along the sides of the ceiling to set up the drapes."

My eyes drift to the large lump of dark velvet sitting in a box next to the table in the middle of the foyer. For an extra, and fairly unreasonable fee, the owners decorate for the client, but to save a few grand, Ciara opted to just rent some of it. Meaning it's up to us three to bring her vision to life.

Dorian disappears down one of the hallways she pointed at, taking the strange heat that's always surrounding him with him.

"Why would you pair us up together?" I prop a hand on my hip and narrow her with a *what-the-hell-were-you-thinking* gaze.

She tries to shrug me off, but I lift my brows, silently

demanding she give me an honest answer. She has to have a good reason for pulling a stunt like this.

Ciara throws her hands up before digging into a bag for more webbing. "Because this is a *team* building exercise. My team needs to bond with the people they'll be working with every day."

I purse my lips before rolling my eyes and grabbing some of the webbing from her hand. I guess that makes sense. She was promoted last month for her strong leadership qualities and then given a department that can't go more than two days without filing an HR complaint about the smallest inconveniences.

They hate each other, and because of that, it's made Ciara miserable. Our weekly girl's night has become daily, and the amounts of wine and relaxing baths she takes are borderline concerning. The wine because any excess alcohol flares her eczema, and the baths because she's taking trips to Lush every week, which is two hours away, and it's dipping into our Spa Saturdays.

I loop some of the webs around the banister and start pulling them out to give it that eerie effect. "And that's the only reason?"

It's not a secret that, at one point, Ciara was hellbent on making me her sister legally through the means of me marrying Dorian. Turns out, he's an ass and I'm a brat, and after many failed attempts at trying to help us to even get along, she finally gave up. Well, it was probably my relationship with Brad that finally ebbed her attempts, but now that he's out of the picture, I wouldn't put it past her to try again.

"Yes." Her voice is an octave higher than a person telling the truth would be.

"*Ciara*," I hiss through clenched teeth.

She holds up her hands in mock surrender. "No, it's not

21

that. There may or may not be a certain someone who's coming, and I'd rather have my brother a little preoccupied instead of focusing on me."

"Someone? You haven't had me deep dive into any socials lately. Also, an employee? How scandalous of you," I joke.

She chews on her bottom lip and flips her twists from her face. "No, not an employee. And yeah, I know. This one's a little different because they work in HR, and it feels like I'm invading their space by snooping."

"Oh, the one you have to talk to almost every day? Jamie, right?"

Ciara nods. "Yup. I feel like something's there, but I'm not sure, and I wanted to use tonight to figure it out. But you know Dorian. He's protective, and I don't need him snooping into something I'm serious about."

"Serious?"

She nods again, and I can't help but relent in my anger over having to keep him preoccupied. "Alright, but this totally adds to the hefty price you already owe me."

She lets out a light laugh. "Deal."

"Hmm, what deals are we making, ladies?" Dorian glides back into the foyer, holding a long ladder over his shoulder as though it's nothing but a sack of potatoes.

The very *uninvited* image of me over his shoulder invades my mind, but I quickly snuff it out.

Dorian clears his throat, and I realize Ciara is too busy thinking of a lie he won't sniff out, forcing me to speak for her. "The deal is that she's getting me hibachi for lunch if I promise not to murder you tonight."

He huffs, setting the ladder up against the wall. "What do I get if *I* behave, baby sis?"

Ciara busies herself with pulling a drape from the box and

handing it to him, causing me to yet again come to the rescue. "Your life. And twelve Canadian sparkling waters."

Dorian lets out a small chuckle before his lips pull down in the corner. "Alright."

Luckily he drops it, and over the next half hour, we throw up Halloween decorations throughout the bottom floor. At some point, Ciara disappears to hide the envelopes in each room, and since she's convinced us to also *play* the game, Dorian and I stay downstairs and set up the table.

"I know for a fact your parents taught you where the salad fork goes, Dorian. Stop putting it down wrong so I have to come behind you and fix it."

He smirks, ignoring me as he puts the name plates next to each setting. "I don't know what you're talking about."

The nastiest scowl I can muster paints my face as I move yet another fork to the correct spot. On the last one, I notice a small brown string sticking out from under the bottom of the plate. I tug it free only to find out it's not a string but the leg of a roach.

A shrill scream escapes me as I throw the insect down and jump back at least a yard, stomping my feet in case it tries to exact revenge on me for dropping it. It only takes half a second, and a deep rumbling laugh, for me to discover it's fake.

My heart hammers behind my sternum, the blood whooshing through my ears so loudly I almost don't hear him.

"Fuck, I love that sound."

My mouth pops open for a quick "fuck off," but Ciara comes out of nowhere, eyes wide with concern as she takes in the scene.

She sighs and gives her brother a much tamer look than I do. "You said you'd behave."

He holds his hands up just like she did when we were

23

setting up the web. "I will when the guests get here. You didn't say anything about before."

Ciara runs a hand over her face, clearly exasperated by her brother's antics as much as I am. "I'm going to pick up lunch for y'all and the dinner for later. Please go outside and have the maze stuff done by the time I get back. Put some space between y'all since I can't supervise you."

He flashes me a look I can't quite discern before nodding. "Will do."

It isn't until she gives him another warning once over and a sympathetic smile to me that she leaves us alone, and I find my voice.

"Grow up," I finally spit. "Seriously. This is getting old."

He shrugs, seeming far too smug for my liking. "I'll grow up when you realize you're twenty-eight and scared of bugs."

"It's a legitimate phobia." I'm all but screaming now.

"Entomophobia," he says lamely, pissing me off more. "Usually caused by a traumatic experience with insects. Remind me again what happened to you?"

I clutch the butter knife in my hand tightly and consider throwing it at him in the hopes my adrenaline makes my throw strong enough to break skin. "*You.* You're what happened to me. You and your fake bugs, you ass."

He whips around the corner in long, heavy strides, surprising me so much I actually take a step back. He leans in way closer than my personal bubble allows and lets his dark eyes roam over my face.

Goose bumps sprout over my bare skin, and I become acutely aware of how little clothing I have on.

"You know what, sunshine? I think you *like it* when I scare you."

My brows furrow in anger, but the air becomes thin, coated

Evelyn

in his warm scent, and my brain becomes too foggy to form a complete sentence. "W-what?"

One side of his lips tilts up in a sinister smirk. "I think you love it when I get that frigid heart of yours pumping and your chest heaving up and down."

Said chest rises and falls faster than it should as I try to capture a full breath. "I—"

"You can fake like you don't," he says, glancing over my face one last time before stepping back. "But I've proved it to you before. It's in the way those nipples of yours draw tight in your shirt. How your cheeks turn a bright pink when you realize how wet you are. Most of all, I *know* you like it because you've never told me to stop."

Without another word, he turns and walks out, humming low and leaving me with my second biggest case of "what the fuck just happened" I've ever experienced.

Dorian

CHAPTER FOUR

L eaving Evelyn in the dining room with her face flushed with that intoxicating mix of frustration and arousal has to be the hardest thing I've ever done.

I'm not really sure what came over me back there. What led me to finally snap.

I could say it's the poetic justice of being back at a Halloween party with her finally single again and me just being the asshole I am. But I know better.

That woman has had me by the throat for too long, and up until now, my only saving grace has been distance. Distance from her smile, her laugh, her fucking thighs that I fantasize about squeezing around my head.

Work has me gone most of the time, and when I'm home, she actively avoids coming over, courtesy of the barrier I put into place a long time ago—the annoying best friend's older brother act. Up until two minutes ago, it's helped keep me from crossing that line.

I mean, it's true I scare her for those intense reactions she always has. But when we were younger, it was because somewhere inside, I already knew. I *knew* that if she gave me the time of day, I'd be a goner.

She was too fucking perfect for her own good. Sweet, thoughtful, fiery, and hard-headed, never bending for me or anyone else. When I'd overhear her and Ciara talking, I couldn't help but be drawn to her, to her opinions, the passion in her voice whenever she spoke.

When she joined the debate team in high school, she'd use me as practice because Lord knows I don't like to lose, and she loved a good opponent. We'd go back and forth, and the light in her eyes acted like a beacon for my fucking ship.

I'd wanted to pluck my heart right out of my chest and give it to her, telling her it was hers whenever she wanted it.

I was head over heels for my baby sister's best friend. A senior in love with a freshman. No matter how right it felt, it was wrong, so I continued my childish antics, annoying her any chance I got.

I'd hoped that in college, the feelings and fascination I felt would fade, that the longer stretches of time without being around her would help me focus on other women.

It worked... until it didn't.

It seems after all these years, my ability to keep her at arm's length has finally disintegrated, and when I found out her douche guy was no longer in the picture? She was mine.

At least, she was supposed to be. But when I went to find her later, she was gone, and a couple of days after that, she was back with her ex.

I don't plan on making that mistake again. Later tonight, I'm letting her know this isn't a game anymore. No more back and forth. Walking around the obvious ends today.

Still caught up in my head, it takes me longer than I'd like to admit to navigate the tall hedges outside of the estate. From the description Ciara gave me, it's over six feet high so that during weddings, guests don't see the bride coming, and the long walk is meant for people to see signs and pictures of the couple. "A walk to forever" is what the maze is called.

Like the lawn, the bushes are fake, so they can take the constant wear and tear of whatever people shove into them and are easy to fix if they get damaged. Maybe that's why I don't think twice about how roughly I shove the massive tarantulas into the bush.

I don't know what it is about being aggressive with inanimate objects, but it does the job of relieving the tight knots in my shoulders. It even helps ease the ache in my slacks that's been there since I saw Evelyn putting together that damn maid outfit.

Since she pretty much grew up with us, I've seen her in everything from baggy shirts and tiny shorts to swimsuits that barely cover anything. Back then, I always made sure to be respectful and look the other way.

Now? I've never wanted to disrespect anyone more.

I haven't even seen her in it yet, and I want to rip that fucking dress to shreds and use the pieces to smother her screams from her tenth orgasm. I want to repurpose the tiny apron to tie her hands together so she can't try and stop me from giving her a dozen more.

I want to show her how everything up until now was to pass the time until I finally got my hands on her.

Until she was mine.

Desire and the rare feeling of apprehension tangle in my chest as I finish setting out the decorations my sister left for the maze. Ciara didn't want her employees to get lost, so the spiders serve as guides to the center, where she's hidden an envelope of clues. It's a large, open space, commonly used for ceremonies.

I put down two dozen Styrofoam gravestones, jab decorative bones into the ground, add in a fog machine, and position a statue of Death with his scythe at the far end.

Being Ciara's brother, I know she's picky as hell, so after scrutinizing my own work and rearranging the props more than I want to, I send a quick picture to make sure she's happy.

Ciara: Move the one in the far back over about six inches. Also, add some webbing. Then it's perfect. Thank you, Dorian.

I give myself a pat on the back because for her to only make two suggestions is like winning a hundred-dollar scratch-off—highly unlikely and pretty fucking awesome.

After moving the gravestone, I realize all the fake cobwebs are inside. I do another quick once over to make sure everything looks good, then grab my bag and make my way back through the maze toward the estate. It connects to the side, which leads me down a long hall opening to the sitting room.

Evelyn's hums flow down the hall like a siren's call to a sailor, and I can't help but follow the sweet sound.

Quietly, I set down the bag and move through the hall until I spot her. Somehow, she's positioned a chair on top of the hearth of the fireplace, balancing on it as she sticks some plastic bats to the stones.

From this angle, she's nothing but long legs and luscious curves that undo my calm nature in a matter of two seconds. Her shirt lifts away from her stockings, rising to show the smooth skin of her lower back. Blood rushes through me, and my heart thuds violently in my chest as I stalk closer to her, unable to resist such a perfect opportunity.

She leans forward, rising on her tiptoes as she tries to put a bat up higher than she should. One leg lifts from the chair, making it wobble slightly, and even with one hand holding the mantel, I see it happen right before it does.

Her content hum morphs into a shriek as the chair tips, and she goes with it, falling in what feels like slow motion. I'm there before she goes down, wrapping my arms around her and balancing us both as the chair clatters against the marble floor.

Naturally, she lets out a more frightened scream when she feels me and slaps my shoulder. "Goddamn it, Dorian."

My eyes widen as I let out a scoff, my hands still firmly in place. "I think a thank you is more appropriate in this context, E."

Her face hardens. "Something tells me if I wouldn't have lost my balance, *you* would have done something to make me fall."

I smirk, loving the way her gaze flits down to my lips. "Maybe, maybe not, but I still saved your ass from hitting the ground."

She rolls her eyes, but I can't help but notice she hasn't moved from my hold. In fact, both of her hands are not only braced on my biceps, but her fingers are tensing around my muscles, making my cock twitch.

"I'm not saying thank you."

"Why?" My voice drops lower as I let myself actually feel her soft body mold into mine. "You hate me that much?"

"Yes." She says it too quickly—too arrogant—for it to be believable.

"Say it," I whisper, leaning an inch closer. "Tell me you hate me."

She tenses beneath me, but her mouth remains pursed in a flat line. She knows it's a challenge, yet for some reason, she can't bring herself to say the words. Her lack of a response, as well as her not moving an inch, makes it impossible not to push her more.

"They say if you hate someone, you should just fuck them," I tell her. "Get all that anger out in a more constructive way."

Her pupils flare, and that bright pink blush I love returns to her cheeks. She can say whatever she likes, but her body doesn't lie, and I see the consideration as soon as it passes over her honey-brown irises. Still, she does her best to act annoyed.

"Fuck off, Dorian." She yanks herself from my arms, and it bothers me how much I resent the emptiness.

I smirk, brushing my hands over my shirt. "Hmm, I'd much rather get *you* off."

Evelyn's mouth pops open, the subtle shock somehow making her even sexier. After a beat, the expression disappears and she waves a dismissive hand. "We both know that would take more time than either of us have."

This makes me laugh. "Sunshine, you'd be on your fifth orgasm before I even got my mouth on you."

Eve throws her head back and lets out an obnoxiously loud cackle. If the sound wasn't goddamn addicting, I might be annoyed. "Fifth? *Fifth*, Dorian? Get serious."

She gingerly wipes under her eyes with her thumb, and I feel the nerve in my jaw suddenly tic. "I'm unsure if it's because you don't think I'm capable or if you think it's impossible because you've never experienced it."

She quickly sobers at my words, and a balloon of satisfaction swells in my chest.

"Wait." Her eyes rove over me to gauge my seriousness, and when she realizes how *dead serious* I am, she takes a step back. "How the fuck would you be able to give me five consecutive orgasms?"

I run a hand through my hair and tilt my head. "Try a dozen or two."

"You're fucking with me right now." She tries to laugh, but it comes out strained and forced. "That's not possible."

I shrug. "Then you've never been with someone like me."

Turning on my heels, I leave the bait and head toward the foyer. I didn't plan on her finding out about my preferences this way, but hey, it works.

My heart picks up its pace the more steps I walk without hers echoing behind me, and for a good thirty seconds, I worry she won't. But then, the tap of her heels relieves tight muscles I didn't even know were tense.

"What do you mean, *someone like you?*"

Keeping my back to her, I go through the bags on the floor until I find the one with the cobwebs. "Someone who gets gratification from giving as many orgasms as possible."

"I—You? How can—"

I turn around, and she lets out a small squeak. I like when she gets frazzled. It makes her fidgety, and I've always wanted to teach her how to control it. "Words, E. Use your words. They're important."

She clamps her mouth shut and huffs, and I enjoy watching her mind try to form a singular sentence. When she finally does, I fucking love how breathy her voice is. "You get off on making someone come as much as you can?"

I nod.

Again, her lips part three times before she shakes her head, and her familiar irritable demeanor takes over. "Well, good for your partners, but I'll have to pass."

Internally, I deflate, but I keep an air of indifference. "Too bad."

"What's too bad?" My sister Ciara appears from the kitchen entrance off to the side, her arms stacked with bags.

Eve shifts to help her. "Nothing. Your brother's up to his usual shit and tricks."

Ah. She thinks I'm fucking with her.

Ciara shoots me a motherly gaze only a Davis woman is capable of. "You promised."

I hold up a hand as I walk backward toward the hall that leads out to the maze. "She's pissed that the man she can't stand just saved her ass from landing in the hospital. Let's hope she's not that clumsy tonight, or else she's probably gonna get murdered first."

"Says the guy who was probably about to scare me, anyway."

I give Evelyn a subtle wink before turning. "Another example of how I know you won't survive tonight."

"Oh, screw you, Dorian," she calls after me before saying something indiscernible to my sister.

If only, sunshine.

Evelyn

CHAPTER FIVE

Five. *A dozen?*

I'm still so caught up on what Dorian just said, I have to ask Ciara to repeat herself twice before I understand the order of events after dinner. Even then, though, I'm admittedly only half-listening.

There's no way he was serious. It has to be another one of those mind games he plays in between scaring me half to death. Like the time when I swallowed gum, and he told me it would tear off pieces of my intestines on its way out.

I was twelve, and somehow the vehemence in his voice was enough to convince me it was true no matter what the internet said. It was a horribly effective trick that succeeded in freaking me the hell out until my mom came home later that night and had a good laugh.

He loves getting in my head, and I have to admit, he's really good at it. I've never been able to pinpoint why it's only ever him who's been able to do it, but because of that, I'm positive this is one of his jokes. A prank born from his boredom. Just another normal day where Dorian fucks with Evelyn.

I sigh to myself, a strange knot forming in my gut. If I'm being honest, I'm not sure if I'm more exasperated at spending

34

energy entertaining the idea that he *may* have the ability to fuck me into oblivion or disappointed it's not actually true.

After placing the soup on the stove to keep it warm, I begin preparing the salads and placing them in the large walk-in refrigerator. Every few minutes, fake thunder rumbles through the walls, and even though I know it's the rain soundtrack playing on the estate's speakers, it makes me bristle every single time.

It's not that I'm scared of storms. It's the notion that at any moment, Dorian might use the sound to hide his steps and time his antics to the drop of thunder, and it has me on edge. Which was probably exactly what he wanted.

Fuck. Tonight is gonna suck.

I try to hum an upbeat song as I finish up the salads, but I end up looking over my shoulder so much, it takes way longer than it should to finish.

The doorbell has rung a good five or six times, and the tune has changed to something low and ominous, making everything worse.

Ugh. Why did I agree to this again?

"How's it going in here, babe?" Ciara's voice appears as I'm popping pans of pasta into the oven.

I close the door and turn around, doing my best to hide the dread I know is etched on my face. "Fine. Almost done. How is everything out there?"

Being her best friend of almost twenty years, I should know she would be able to sense something was up. Or maybe I just suck at masking how I feel. "What's wrong?"

I shake my head. "I'm good."

Ciara grumbles a curse to herself before pursing her lips. "Girl, what did he do?"

A bitter laugh escapes my lips. "To be fair, it's not *just* him. It's this place."

I wave a hand around at nothing in particular. I feel like such a fucking kid for being scared of a mansion adorned with basic Halloween decorations.

But that's the thing about Ciara. She has never, not once, judged me for being an adult scaredy-cat. Unlike my now ex-boyfriend, she's always reassured me that everyone has something they're afraid of, and mine just so happens to be things that go bump in the night.

Hell, back in school, she was down to slap someone if they laughed at me for flipping out when a love-bug got too close. She watches Christmas movies with me on Halloween and never mutters a word when I literally sprint into the next room after turning off the lights.

She's the best... when she's not asking me to basically throw myself in immersion therapy.

Ciara gives me one of her mother's empathic smiles before nodding. "How about this? Can you help Dorian pass out the food, then I'll have an Uber pick you up? Just stay in the kitchen and dining areas, and *I'll* be the one to walk you out."

God, why have you forsaken me?

It only takes a second for me to make my decision. This woman has been there for me through bugs, my parents' horrific attempt at co-parenting, and my own sloppy breakup. There's no way I'm not sucking it up and dealing for one evening.

"No. You deserve to have a brother-free night and figure these things out with Jamie."

Ciara does a shit job at stifling the huge grin that splits across her face, so she masks it by giving me a quick, appreciative hug. "Are you sure? We both know he's gonna fuck with you."

This makes me scoff. "Oh, girl, what's new? He actually already started."

Her head falls back with an exaggerated sigh. "Seriously?"

"Yep. He was talking shit earlier about giving women an insane amount of orgasms."

Ciara's face twists like she's tasted a lemon as she stirs the soup before serving herself a small sample ramekin. "Well, it's not a lie, but he shouldn't be teasing you about it."

It takes her tasting the soup, making a satisfied sound of approval, and her finishing the small bowl before I find the words to form a response. "He wasn't lying?"

She shakes her head.

A strange sensation moves low in my stomach. "He can give a woman a dozen *consecutive* orgasms?"

"It's a fact I absolutely *despise* knowing, but yep."

"There's no fucking way."

Ciara makes a grumbling noise as she rinses her dish and puts it in the sink. "It definitely is, and I'm very disturbed that I not only know that about my big brother but that you're forcing me to think about it. I tucked that trauma into the deepest part of my mind, hopeful it'd never resurface again."

"Wait." I shake my head back and forth as if it will make invisible puzzle pieces suddenly fall into place. "I have too many questions."

"Well, you better settle on, like, two. I have to go entertain those people, or they'll be using napkins to file complaints with Jamie."

With the way she talks about the employees, I don't doubt it. Tugging my bottom lip between my teeth, I rack through the million and one questions I have and settle on the most important one.

"*How* did you find out?"

"Ugh. Okay. TMI story, but it was a while back when I went with him to SoCal, when he was scouting. There was a party I really wanted to go to with some of his old friends, and unfortunately, after a stop at a sketchy taco shop, I was stuck in one of the private bathrooms for, like, an hour. At some point, he must have brought someone up, and—"

She stops, her entire body shuddering as she makes a retching noise. "He didn't stop 'til she threw in the towel at like number fifteen, and I was helplessly stuck on the toilet the entire twenty minutes."

Fifteen times in twenty minutes? My jaw is nearly on the floor when she laughs. It's not a funny type of laugh, but a sad *laugh so I'm not vomiting all over the counter* type of laugh. "Close your mouth before you catch a fly. You didn't have to live through it. I had to increase my therapy sessions for like three months before I was able to look at him again. "

"So he wasn't done?" I don't bother trying to smother the shock in my voice. To me, coming twice is like finding a damn unicorn. Fifteen sounds made up.

Ciara shakes her head. "Pleasure Doms are scary, Eve. They want their partner to be a pile of mush on the floor. Also, can we please change the subject? I'm getting nauseous."

"Wait, wait, wait. Back up. You're telling me your brother is a pleasure Dom?"

I've heard the term before—albeit, it was only a vague discussion once back in college— but I'd honestly chalked it up to being... what's more impossible than finding a unicorn? Yeah, whatever that is.

"Girl, stay with me. Yes." She takes a new ramekin and fills it up. "Also, even sick to my stomach, I can't stop eating this. I'm either really hungry or this soup is hella good."

I shake my head. "No, it's good."

"Hmmm," she hums around the dish. "Anything else? I gotta get out there. Please say no."

I want to tell her yes, but suddenly, I can't even think of one word. I'm too busy considering taking her brother up on his offer of a hate fuck.

No. I can't do that.

Well, maybe.

It would just be one time. One and done.

Get all the pent-up anger out and move on.

It's not like I haven't thought about it before. A lot.

No.

I go back and forth as she rinses out the second ramekin. "Alright, well, if you change your mind about leaving, just let me know. I'm sure there's someone else I can pair him up with."

As if on cue, Dorian appears in the tall doorway.

He's dressed in his butler costume, and I'm pretty sure he bought it from the sexy adult section, two end-caps away from where I got mine. His tailcoat is snug, clinging to the lean muscles he earned from eight years of being a wide receiver. The front is buttoned up three-quarters of the way, and the top of his chest is slightly hidden by his loose-fitting tie where there's a glint of a small silver chain around his neck.

Yeah, maybe just once. If it turns out it's not true, I'll have ammunition for the next two years *at least.*

"They're looking for you, sis. Someone named Jamie says everyone is here."

"Oh." Ciara perks up, brushing off her slacks. "I'll get everyone seated, and y'all can bring out the waters."

I nod, but when my eyes shift from her back to Dorian, I realize he's livid. There's an aura of fury radiating off him, and my defenses go on high alert. The fine hairs on my neck rise, and my heart starts pumping faster.

Why do I kind of like that look?

When Ciara disappears through the door, I immediately address it. It probably means he's finally about to come at me about the cayenne pepper, and I don't have time for more shit piled on top of everything else. "What's your deal?"

His dark eyes scan over my frame twice before he gestures behind him. "What was she talking about?"

The air becomes thinner with the drop in his tone. I've never heard him so...commanding. "First off, mind your business. Second, I'm not leaving, if that's what you're asking."

"Oh, I know you're not."

My head jerks back, surprise mixing with another emotion I can't quite place. "But if I wanted to—"

"But you're not." His cockiness makes me want to punch a hole in the wall.

"Yeah, that's already been established, but the offer is there if I want it."

Dorian takes a heavy step toward me, and I suck in a breath. He stops and shakes his head with a smirk. "Why is it an option, E?"

I shrug, giving him my back as I grab the empty pitchers and begin filling them with ice. "Because she knows you're probably going to give me a heart attack before the night's over."

Though I can no longer see him, I can feel the heat of his gaze. Before, it was always annoying, but now, it's somehow electrifying. My skin tingles as he moves closer, and by the time I feel his warm breath coast along my shoulder, I'm damn near vibrating.

"How about this, sunshine?" His deep voice rumbles down my spine, sending a wave of shivers through me. "I promise to only do what you ask me to. If you don't want me to scare you, I won't. If you don't want me to trick or tease you, I won't."

Though no part of him touches me, I somehow feel him move closer, just like the night of the Halloween party. And just like then, I *want* him to, even if it's just the briefest contact.

I need to know if this is adrenaline or something more. Something so knotted and tight from years of back and forth that only one thing could relieve it.

"But if there's something you'd like me to do, I can."

"Like what, Dorian?" Unlike him, my voice is much softer, the slight crack giving away my nerves. I clear my throat, pouring water into one of the glasses and regaining some of my composure. "What could you possibly do for me?"

He chuckles low before slipping his calloused fingers over mine and tipping my hand too far, causing the glass to overflow. "Show you what you're capable of."

Then, without a single word, he slips away, leaving me with a mess on the counter and between my thighs.

Evelyn

CHAPTER SIX

Something tells me I'm about to bite off more than I can chew if I say yes to whatever Dorian just offered.

If I wanted to be hypothetical and take having to clean up a mess *he* caused as any indication of what tonight will be like, I'm already annoyed. But if I look past it and consider his words... well, for some unknown reason, it has me wanting things I normally wouldn't think twice about.

Show you what you're capable of.

Now knowing what he enjoys, I'm sure he meant how many orgasms he can wring out of me, and that thought alone is making my skin feel as if it's on fire.

I shouldn't want to experience anything with this man. The very same man who is literally the reason for ninety percent of my fears as an adult. But I'd be lying if I said I hadn't considered it more than a couple of times. I mean, who hasn't wanted to bang their best friend's older brother? I'm pretty sure it's a thing.

Am I really considering this?

I mean... what's one night? I doubt he'll be able to do anything drastic anyway, since we're playing Ciara's game and can be interrupted at any moment. Still, the temptation to give in, even if just this once, is too enticing not to consider.

Letting my teeth sink into my bottom lip, I tray up the waters and saunter into the dining area.

When I enter the room, I immediately feel the shift in the air. It's stifling. If not for Dorian standing stock still in the corner, it's the guests glaring at each other as if they'd love nothing more than to commit a very real crime tonight.

The low light of the chandelier illuminates the table and its occupants in an eerie glow, further highlighting the anger etched in their scowls. It's clear from the stiff shoulders and sideway glances that whoever their 'work friend' is isn't sitting next to them.

The only thing going for the group is the clear dedication to whatever character they've been assigned. I'm more than positive it's so they can one-up each other, but I have to admit, I'm impressed.

Ciara, of course, had to switch up the character names since they have more than the six from the movie, but also didn't want anyone complaining they weren't one of the original cast. So, we stayed up one night and crafted new ones. It was a little tedious at first since she wanted to give them personalities as well, but after a while, it was kind of fun coming up with profiles.

Now, seeing them in all their glory makes the long night worth it.

I decide to over-concentrate on each of the characters in front of me as I pass out their waters. If not to see my hard work come to fruition, it's so I can avoid eye contact with Dorian, whose gaze is burning the side of my face.

Ciara and Jamie get their glasses first. Lady Lavender and Detective Danube. Jamie's blond hair is slicked back, contrasting well against the misty blue suit.

Next are Mistress Mint, Colonel Cream, and Sir Saffron. Yeah, the names are definitely unnecessary and ridiculous, but they're meant to be fun, which this group clearly needs a little more of in their lives.

Mint has on a gorgeous spaghetti-strap gown that clings to her like a second skin. Cream is in a three-piece off-white suit, and judging from the dark roots in his ash-tinted hair, also must've done a little temporary spray to bring it all together. Saffron went a little more subtle with the color combo, opting for a pair of rusted-colored slacks and suspenders over a button-down. He's handsome. His jaw is sharp, the stubble decorating it stops just under his high cheekbones, while his dark hair is mussed as though he's run his hands through it a few times, and—

"Let me help you with that." Dorian's sudden appearance next to me makes me jolt slightly.

When I lift a questioning brow, he shoots me a gaze similar to the one he did in the kitchen when he thought I might be leaving. Only this one is a little different. There's a bit more fire lightning up his irises.

Jealousy?

I internally scoff as I walk around the table, letting him unload the tray and pass out the drinks. There's no way Dorian Davis would be jealous of anyone. The man is as self-assured and cocky as they come. No. It's more probable he was impatient with how slow I was going.

We make our rounds quickly, and only Mrs. Magenta and Professor Periwinkle utter a thanks.

"I'll be right back with the salads," I say to no one in particular before retreating to the kitchen.

"Tough crowd." Dorian's close voice informs me he's decided to follow me.

Rather than throw some smartass remark back at him, my shoulders relax a little. "It wasn't just me, right?"

He shakes his head. "No. If I had to go to work and deal with that every day, I wouldn't make it a week."

"Well, that's because you're used to yelling at people for a living," I point out, opening the refrigerator and drawing out the prepared salads.

"I do the opposite, actually. I'm a scouter, not a coach. My job is to make players feel comfortable in taking a leap of faith."

Even though he's talking about football, I can't help but apply it to what I'm already considering doing with him. "And what if it's the wrong choice?"

Dorian steps closer, the heat from his body enveloping me, warming my core despite the fridge's cool air. "I'm never the wrong choice, sunshine."

A wave of tingles shoots down my arms before settling low in my belly. I want to question when the hell Dorian became so... *alluring*, but the answer becomes obvious with little thought.

Ever since that Halloween, he's never come on to me. Never laid on the Davis charm I've heard so much about. He's kept me at arm's length—which wasn't hard, considering I got back with my safety net of an ex—and never pushed the envelope past a flirty comment here or there.

Now? Something's changed, or perhaps finally been set free, and I'm not gonna lie, I'm *really* considering taking the bait.

"How do you know no one's ever regretted it?" My question comes out with an appropriate amount of sass, but I'm sure if he listens hard enough, he can hear my heart hammering in my rib cage.

Dorian moves closer, lifting his hand slowly to run the pad

of his thumb along my jaw. A shiver racks through me, even though I try to narrow my eyes in indignation.

The corner of his lips curl up as he removes his hand, grabbing a salad from behind me. "Because I deliver exactly what I tell them I will."

That statement shouldn't make my blood rush to my clit, but it does, and I squirm—actually squirm—beside him. It makes the opinionated goddess in my head turn around and dig her feet into the ground.

I grab two salad bowls and dip beneath his raised arm to my tray. "Words are just that, Dorian. Words. They mean shit when it comes to proving anything and usually only set people up for disappointment. So, if I were you, I'd tone it down."

Unlike the smart remark I expect from him, he grants me a lopsided grin and shrugs. "No truer words have even been spoken. I hope they taste good when I jam them down your pretty little throat later."

Something between a huff and laugh falls from my very open mouth as I stand cemented to the kitchen floor.

I'm one thousand percent sure that's not supposed to turn me on, but holy shit, my entire pussy is now throbbing.

Shit.

My libido is doing a number on my ability to think properly, and if I don't put some damn space between him and me, I know my horny ass is going to give in. At this point, I think I'm more scared of actually enjoying it and wanting it to continue than I am about some awkward aftermath.

My mind flirts with different ideas as I turn my back and finish stacking a few salads on the tray. Maybe I could make it interesting and solve my dilemma of having to decide myself with a simple game. We both know he won't be able to say no to that.

I nod to myself as I lift the tray and turn around, but I find Dorian already gone. The odd sensation of missing his presence is what makes me question myself all over again.

I need a drink.

Dorian

CHAPTER SEVEN

This time, when she walks into the dining area, I stay out of sight in the hallway adjacent to the table. I told myself I'd go all out with this, but in doing so, I'm forcing my own walls to drop, and parts of myself she's never seen are flooding out faster than I can reel them in.

First, it was the dick jealousy move when she was passing out water. It wasn't my place to step in like that, but fuck, it took everything in my soul not to take away orange-pant guy's ability to see after the way he was eye-fucking her. When she reciprocated a little bit of that visual flirting, my damn vision went red. It reminded me of all the times I had to refrain from saying or doing anything because of that tool she was with all those years.

Then, there was touching her in the kitchen. The impulse was so strong I couldn't stop myself no matter how much my mind screamed I was doing too much, too fast. But the warm, smooth feel of her skin under my thumb was enough to eliminate every doubt in my mind. Every thought that said this shouldn't be happening.

She's not just my kid sister's friend anymore. Nor is she the forbidden fruit.

No, she's the exact opposite now. She's a grown-ass woman I want beneath me. Who I want writhing and screaming and so fucking lost, the only thing she can remember is the three syllables needed to say my name.

My gaze follows Eve as she passes out the salads. Every time she reaches her hand up to grab a plate from the tray, her skirt lifts the inch needed to showcase the tops of her thighs poking out from her thigh highs. I want to sink my fucking teeth into the flesh and mark it so the orange pants guy knows she's unavailable.

Actually, so *every* man knows she's not available.

Because I already know one night with her won't be enough. It will open up something that's long overdue, and I know me and my greed.

Once I have her, I'm not letting go, and I fully intended to show her why she should belong to me. Why it was always supposed to end with us.

I continue to watch her set down the dishes, and when Ciara gives E a look that's heavy code for *help me*, she responds with an empathic smile, and I have to stifle a laugh.

I love my baby sister, and I've always tried to encourage her in every aspect of her life, but I really, *really* wanna hit her with an I-told-ya-so. When she first asked for my thoughts on this whole "team building" exercise, I flat-out told her it'd be a disaster. Not because I didn't think she was capable of hosting a bad-ass party, but because the complaints she's had me read in her email are downright nasty.

These people hate each other, and *not* in a way that could lead to hate sex, but in a vile, put-sugar-in-your-gas-tank type way. They don't stop bickering. The pettiness is the kind of shit you'd expect in high school, and the comments they throw at each other are the ones I hear on the line of scrimmage before players smash their bodies into each other.

Chapter 7

Still, as I move down the hall and back into the kitchen, I can't help but consider how I could make tonight better for her. Part of me hopes these people actually have fun because, honestly, once E and I are alone, I don't think I'll be able to come up for air until she's tapped out.

I lean my hip into the counter, next to the soup as Evelyn reenters the kitchen. Her brows are turned up, exasperation clear in her delicate features. She's so fucking beautiful, I swear there's an aura around her. That's where she gets her nickname, sunshine. The woman glows even when she's not trying.

When she looks up and notices me, she's quick about trying to conceal the sudden tenseness in her shoulders and the uptick in her breathing.

But I notice it. I notice everything about her.

She tries to ignore my presence and moves next to me, ladling soup into bowls.

"Make yourself useful and pass these out." She shoves the first one into my chest, but not hard enough to cause it to slosh over the sides.

Even in her periphery, I know she sees the wide smirk painting my face. "I can make myself plenty useful, E. Just tell me what you want me to do."

She scoffs, filling another bowl. "What the hell has gotten into you?"

"What do you mean?"

She chews on her bottom lip but doesn't give in to any temptation she might have about looking at me. She's known me too long and knows exactly what I'm doing.

Evelyn has always been an easy read. It's why she dropped her dreams of being a lawyer. She's well aware the second she gives me those honey eyes, I'll call her bluff—she's not annoyed by my presence, she *wants* it. I'd even go so far as to say she craves it.

50

After another second, she takes a calming breath, but from the way a nerve tics in her jaw, I'm positive it had the opposite effect. She's so close to me, I'm sure my scent is in every particle of the air she took in.

"You're playing a game I have no intention of joining."

"Hmmm." My low rumble fills the small space between us as I take the bowl from her hand. "And what gives you the impression this is some kind of game?"

Again, she has to fight the urge to look at me, though her eyes do flash over briefly, and her grip tightens around the ladle as she scoops. "Dorian, let's be real for a second."

I hold my hand out to accept the next bowl. "Let's."

She scrunches up her nose at my response before rolling her eyes. "Since when does having hate sex with your baby sister's best friend sound appealing?"

This makes me chuckle. I thought she was gorgeous when we were kids, but a three-year age gap back then was a big deal. I had to force my seventeen-year-old mind to see her fourteen-year-old self as nothing more than cute.

When I came home from college my junior year and realized she was making college plans over the summer? Well, there were more than a few nights where images in my head were of her. Still, I was able to keep my distance and respect her relationship, no matter how much I hated the guy.

Finding ways to continue respecting it only got harder when we all graduated, and she bought the townhouse a few units down. She was over all the damn time, and every petty argument we had ended with me wanting to turn her over my knee and finger fuck her through at least eight orgasms.

I remember the worst argument that had me so heated I almost risked it all. It was the day I pushed her over the edge and debated her on the merits of who should have won a bake-off show until her whole body was a deep shade of red. She was

51

so damn mad, her body was shaking, and all I wanted to do was bury my face in her cunt and see if she was as wet as I was hard.

"It was the day you threw the remote at my face."

Her arched brows cinch together briefly before it clicks. Then, her face morphs into something mixed with shock and pride. She likes knowing I wanted her even when she chucked a piece of plastic at me. "You wanted to fuck me then?"

I nod, filling the tray with the last bowl that will fit. "I wanted to do a lot more than that, sunshine."

Eve's breath catches, and I decide fighting the temptation to kiss her isn't worth it anymore. Lifting one hand, I reach for her jaw, but she tilts it slightly, causing my fingers to brush against her neck.

Her eyes flare, and my cock pulses, but when I lean down to finally claim her perfect mouth, a sudden rumble of thunder shakes the kitchen speakers. The unexpected sound makes her jerk, spilling some of the soup I hadn't realized she was holding.

She hisses out as it drips over her hand and onto the floor between our feet. When my eyes connect with hers, desire licks at my spine as I take in her hooded gaze.

Without thinking, I lift her hand, take the bowl, then watch her reaction as I suck her two soiled fingers into my mouth. The fucking gasp she lets out is enough to make my dick weep.

The slightly sweet, creamy taste of the soup is nothing compared to her reaction. The pure need radiating off of her as she watches me with fixed eyes as I clean her digits.

My tongue whirls around them, diving between her knuckles and around the rings circling her fingers. When I suck my way up, her lashes flutter closed, a soft moan escaping her.

I'm two seconds away from saying fuck the dinner, but the

click of incoming heels jolts us from the bubble we've found ourselves in.

Ciara appears in the entryway, a look of despair wrinkling the corner of her eyes. "Why did I think this was a good idea?"

Eve is the first to move, and it takes more restraint than I care to admit not to wrap my hand around her waist and draw her back to me.

"It's gonna be fine. Once the game starts, they'll be so excited to one-up each other, they won't give you any trouble." I lift the first tray and nod to her. "I promise it'll work out."

Ciara mumbles a quick, "I hope so," after me as I disappear back into the dining area to serve the soup. When I come back for the second tray, Evelyn's little wall is back in place.

"Took you long enough. Take this one so I can start plating the pasta."

I roll my eyes playfully and release a small chuckle when she tries to give me a stern look. How is she even cuter when she thinks she's scolding me? "Do you think these people are vacuums? Give them a minute to finish the soup first."

She shakes her head, pushing the tray into my hands. "Ciara gave me a schedule. She said if they always have something in front of them, there's no room for them to get bored and start arguing."

It makes sense in theory, but part of me is under the distinct impression Eve's trying to make sure we aren't alone together for longer than a few seconds.

Her futile attempt to prolong the inevitable is short-lived, though, because after serving the soup and then following behind quickly with the main dish, the only thing standing in the way of me finally having her is the damn lights going out.

Evelyn

CHAPTER EIGHT

W hen the lights go out, my entire body becomes a lump of lead. Fight or flight has completely left the building, and instead, fear has tightened around my nerves and locked me in place.

The tender muscle in my ribcage beats out of control, while every breath I take is no longer sufficient enough to fill my lungs.

I knew this was going to happen. Ciara made sure to tell me down to the second when Dorian would be cutting out the lights. But now, stuck in the thick darkness like a prehistoric animal in tar, I'm made acutely aware of how little I was ready for it.

To make matters exponentially worse, the fine hairs on the back of my neck rise when I realize I'm no longer the only one occupying the kitchen. As if I'm one of those idiot characters in the movies, I call out, basically beckoning the other party to move closer to me.

"Ciara?"

No answer. My nerves begin to tingle as I feel the heavy presence move closer.

"Dorian, this isn't funny. The lights were only supposed to be off for thirty seconds."

Again, no response.

My chest starts to move faster, the air even thinner than it was a moment ago. What if it's one of those grumpy-ass employees looking to expel a little pent-up anger?

Shit.

The idea is enough to spur me into action, but the second my foot lifts from the ground, a familiar touch glides up the outside of my thigh.

I suck in a sharp breath, a scream tickling the edge of my tongue, but before the sound comes out, a strong hand clamps down on top of my mouth, *hard*.

My blood whooshes through my ears, Dorian's warm, woodsy smell doing wild things to my body while the sheer panic of the dark does a number on everything else.

"Shhh," he teases. "I don't want you screaming just yet."

The double meaning behind his words slinks right down to my core.

"Tell me, E. Have you ever laid in bed, looking off into the dark, scared of what might be lurking out of sight?"

I swallow hard, my breath even harder to catch now. When I nod, I can practically *feel* the smile split across his face.

"And have you ever spread these legs with thoughts of me being there? Waiting for you in that darkness?"

My thighs clench together, heat flaring through my body, making me grateful he can't see me.

I can't answer that. To tell him the truth would be admitting things I haven't even admitted to myself.

My head shakes slightly, and he laughs. "I never took you for a liar, sunshine."

Suddenly, the idle hand next to my thigh moves and slides

across to the inside. I shudder beneath the faint touch, my body moving closer to him of its own accord. He's so close to the aching throb, I couldn't care less about the muffled voices growing louder outside of the kitchen as people start moving around.

"Have you ever touched yourself while imagining me, Evelyn?"

The way his tongue curls around the letters of my name is all I need to push whatever little indecision I had left to the wayside. Now, it's replaced with the incessant need to hear him say my name like that, over and over again.

"Have you ever circled this clit and wished it was me?"

I nod, too far gone to lie anymore, and he rewards my honesty by flicking a finger out, brushing against the spot I need him most. The sensation of the connection spears through my nerves, coaxing out a needy whimper I don't bother trying to stop.

His fingers tense around my mouth as he leans in, skimming his nose along the side of my jaw, all the way back to my ear. I shiver against him, pressing myself closer.

"Good." His hand disappears from my mouth and grips my jaw, turning it to the side to give him full access to the column of my neck. My nerves vibrate as I wait for him to do something —*anything*—but in the next second, he's gone.

You have got to be shitting me.

"*Dorian*," I whisper-shout through the dark space, fear and excitement now mixing with the classic annoyance he always causes. Not a game, my ass.

I bite down on the inside of my cheek so hard, a tangy copper taste coats my tongue. I can't *believe* I fell for his stupid-ass trick.

There's no way I shouldn't have seen it coming. It was way too random not to see the red flags.

A tightness pinches across my chest, and I rub at the

foreign ache. This is exactly why I've kept my distance from him in the first place. He's good with words, both when he's trying to scare me and in the occasional instances where he's actually thoughtful, and I took his bait without a second thought. Because for once, I thought maybe the underlying attraction wasn't one-sided, that I didn't have to feel stupid for it.

I grumble to myself as I grip the kitchen counter behind me and wait. Finally, the lights flicker on, and only a second passes before a shrill scream echoes throughout the hall.

It's so loud and unbelievably authentic that goose bumps rise along my arms, and I actually wince while running out, finding everyone in the grand room with the fireplace.

All the employees are standing in a loose circle, their eyes glued to the floor where Jamie is lying post-mortem. Obvious fake blood splatter has been strategically placed, only touching the detective's uniform and none of the very expensive furniture.

Ciara stands with her hand covering her mouth, theatrical-level fear etched in her features. "There's been a murder!"

Her employees all exchange looks, and for the first time since they've arrived, a majority of them look slightly entertained. The buzz fuels Ciara as she takes a handkerchief from between her breasts and makes a show of wiping under her eyes.

"No one can leave until we inform the authorities," she announces, adopting a sudden Southern accent. At least, I think it's sudden, as I've been so wrapped up in Dorian that I haven't heard her address anyone before now.

"We can't." Speak of the devil, and he shall appear. The man himself appears from a back hallway, holding up his cell phone. "The storm must have taken down a tower because there's no reception."

"So what will we do?" she goes on, looking around until her eyes land on me.

That's my cue.

I perk up, dusting my maid skirt before adopting a soft-spoken tone. "The killer must be one of them. You must find out who they are before they kill again, Lady Lavender."

Ciara nods, snapping at her brother. "Yes. We must work together to find out who would commit such a heinous crime and stop them before they kill anyone else."

On cue, Dorian passes out slips of paper to each partici-pant, including myself. I avoid his gaze, but when our fingers brush against one another, the tingle is hard to ignore.

"Alright. Now that you all have your recording sheets, let me explain how the game will proceed."

Ciara goes on to explain that everyone will be paired up, and, authentic to the movie, will all draw straws to determine who is partnered with whom. After that, they will be assigned to a room, where they have fifteen minutes to search for clues, which are hidden in a manila envelope somewhere inside. If they find it, they'll need to go through it, mark any notes on their sheets, and put the envelope back exactly where they found it.

When the fifteen minutes are up, they'll hear a rumble of thunder and a crack of lightning, indicating it's time to rotate to the next room. On the back of the recording paper, there's a small map which directs them to the next room.

It's simple enough, and honestly, if a plethora of different emotions weren't currently battling it out in my stomach like gladiators, I'd be way more excited.

She asks if anyone has any questions, and only one person raises their hand. It's a stout gentleman in a pea-green suit with a face that reminds me of the grumpy cat meme. "Is there a chance we may be paired up with the killer?"

Ciara nods. "Yes, but I decided to do things differently than the instructions for this. Instead of telling the killer who they are, I want them to figure it out along with their partner. It makes it a tad more suspenseful. If the killer discovers they, themselves, are the murderer, they can *kill* their partner."

She puts air quotes around the word kill, but I see a few smirks that pass over some of her employees.

Geesh, I feel bad for her.

"And if the partner figures it out first, they have to find me before being killed. Everyone got it?"

A small round of murmured yeses echo in the space before she holds out a hand for Jamie, who conveniently rises from the dead. "For obvious reasons, I will be paired with Jamie, and we'll be walking around, overseeing the game, ensuring each of you are playing by the rules. No sharing of information under any circumstances."

Again, they all agree before lining up and drawing straws. The vast majority of pairs are clearly pissed about their partner but, after a little reassurance, go to their first assigned room.

When no one is left but Dorian and me, Ciara tells us to start in room eight.

I look at the map, and when I realize where room eight is, panic sweeps over me. "That's the attic."

Ciara nods, already trying to move into the hallway. "Yep."

"Ciara—"

"Let's go, sunshine." Dorian swoops his arm around my back and ushers me toward the stairs.

I hit his arm, moving to the side. "Don't touch me, ass."

He smirks, pocketing his hand and winking at me. *Winking.* "Funny. I don't remember you saying that in the kitchen. In fact, I think it was the opposi—"

"What?" Ciara tilts her head, a gleam too damn jolly for my liking passing through her eyes.

Lord knows I don't need her thinking the long-lost dream of us being sisters is still a possibility, so I wave her off and tug Dorian's sleeve in the direction of the stairs. "Nothing. He's doing what he does best."

"Which is?" Dorian asks from behind me.

"Being an asshole," I huff before starting the climb. "Now come on, before I accidentally break a rule and kill you prematurely."

Evelyn

CHAPTER NINE

I think everyone has toxic traits. Characteristics about themselves they know are borderline petty and unnecessary but make them feel better.

Mine just so happens to be passive aggressiveness. It's a skill I picked up from my mother, but definitely perfected it when I met Dorian. Don't get me wrong, verbal sparring with him is pleasant, but there's something about consuming the last one of his favorite drinks or parking behind his car, knowing he has to leave for work, that brings me so much joy.

Right now? Well, I'm walking up a narrow flight of stairs, my skirt bouncing from the intense sway of my hips, and I'm one thousand percent sure that with my height from the heels, he's getting a good show.

The show being my ass with red lace fabric covering my cunt.

He wants to be a tease? I can definitely play that game just as well. If not better.

I'm so distracted with making sure I seem unbothered, I don't notice the flurry of butterflies in my stomach until we actually make it to the attic door.

My hands turn clammy as I reach for the handle, and my heart has once again found a home in the base of my throat.

Shit, I should've let him go first.

No. My inner warrior goddess turns her head again. I shouldn't have. He needs to be punished for that stunt in the kitchen, and what better way than showing him what he missed out on?

With a grunt too sensual to be mistaken as anything other than a soft moan, I hoist the door open. It flings forward a little too quickly, and I stumble, causing Dorian to step up and jerk me back into him.

Oh. *Oh.*

His massive bulge pressing into my ass lets me know just how much my pettiness affected him. At least, that's what I tell myself, until I look up and see a life-sized clown brandishing a blade coated in something red.

A scream rips from my throat, but Dorian's hand clamps over my mouth, muffling the burning noise tearing up my esophagus. "It's not real, E. Calm down."

Adrenaline and dread wind together tight in my abdomen, threatening to send me into cardiac arrest. I shake him off, quickly moving around the statue. "Why is this up here?"

"All the stuff Ciara could have rented is up here. But since she was going for the mystery party, she didn't need any of it."

I huff, my eyes bouncing over the boxes of gore. Some are full of bloody bones, other assortments of masks, furry eight-legged spiders, and so much more I could've spent the night *not* seeing.

I dodge a string of what I suspect is real cobwebs and nearly scream all over again when I look up and see my reflection staring back at me.

"*Shit.*" My heart hammers, slapping against my ribcage painfully as Dorian appears behind me.

"Let me ask you something." His eyes are trained on me through the reflective glass, his gaze hooded and angry, and something so close to pure hunger, my core tenses all over again. "Did you think that was cute, E?"

His voice rumbles against the curve of my neck, sprouting goose bumps over my arms. Still, I manage to feign ignorance. "No idea what you mean."

I try to take a step forward, but he wraps his arm around my waist, locking me in place. "Parading up those stairs and shoving that pretty little pussy in my face."

His fingers grip the top of my skirt before he makes a fist, bunching the already short fabric up, exposing my entire thigh. As soon as I figure out what's happening, it's too late.

Dorian's free hand comes down on my ass hard, making me yelp and jerk in his hold.

The sharp pain is very short-lived, though, melting into an intoxicating pleasure that doesn't even seem real. When he rubs at the tender skin, he asks again, "Do you think it's fun to tease me?"

I swallow, the response I had ready fizzles into ash, making my mouth dry. How can his voice be so... delicious? It's stern and commanding, yet soft and sensual.

I start to open my mouth, but the sharp pain rings out again as his hand comes down for a second blow.

"*Fuck.*" Why does that feel so good?

"I asked you a question, sunshine. Do you enjoy teasing me?"

"Yes," I breathe honestly, my chest heaving.

"Hmm." His low treble vibrates my back, the sound sinking into my bloodstream.

"You did it first," I point out, barely able to see him from the narrow slits my eyes have become.

He lowers his head, brushing his lips along the curve of my

neck. The sensation is intoxicating, and suddenly, whatever happened in the kitchen no longer matters. Just so long as he doesn't stop now, I'm willing to overlook it.

"What I did in the kitchen wasn't teasing you, Eve. I was simply asking a question."

I scoff, pushing my hips backward so his erection digs into my ass. A low hissing sound escapes his clenched teeth, and he releases my waist, trailing his hand up to my throat. His fingers circle around it, closing just tight enough to make me suck in a breath.

"If you want me to show you what it looks like to be teased by me, I'm more than happy to oblige."

My eyes flare, opening again to see him clearly in the mirror. His gaze bores into mine, and there's a promise burning in them that I want to let consume me whole. Before I can talk myself out of it, I nod.

A smirk curls the ends of his lips, and it's when his foot kicks the door behind us closed that I know I did, in fact, bite off more than I could chew.

Still holding me by the throat, he lets his free hand coast along my body. His fingers ghost over the swell of my cleavage that's pushed up perfectly thanks to the bodice of the outfit. My nipples pebble under his touch, the thin fabric doing nothing to hide them.

He lets out a satisfied rumble before pinching each one between his fingers. "Have you ever come from these?"

I shake my head, moaning as he tugs on one softly. "No."

"Good," he murmurs before moving lower.

He walks his fingers down my torso, taking his time to note which spots make me wriggle or squirm. "I love how fucking sensitive you are."

That's the thing—I'm not. No one has ever made my body feel as if it's damn near two seconds from bursting into flames, let alone making me want so much *more*. More touching, caressing, more teasing. It's not me. It's *him*.

His fingers move lower, dipping into the top of my skirt. "Are you dripping for me?"

I shake my head as much as his firm grip allows, trying to put on an air of indifference. "Nope."

He chuckles again, skimming his finger lightly over the waistband of the lace. "You're a terrible liar, sunshine."

I add extra emphasis as I roll my eyes, but they quickly squeeze shut when he slides his hand lower, placing the rough pad of his finger exactly where I need it. Jolts of pleasure ripple up through my nerves, and I shift in this hold, desperate for more friction.

"Tell me something, E. How many times have you come with my name on your lips?"

"Never," I answer quickly, and this time, it's the truth. While he may get it out of me that I've fucked myself to thoughts of him, I never let imaginary him make me finish.

I couldn't. It would breach a line I knew wouldn't ever happen, not to mention my general disdain for the man was enough to keep us in our respective places. But the more I melt under his touch, the more I wonder what real hate is and if I ever truly hated him at all.

Maybe what I felt for him was more like a secret longing that I forced to shift into annoyance. I needed to make myself think I hated him because he wasn't the safe choice. He was the wild card.

Now, the closer his finger gets to my entrance, the more I wonder if wild is exactly what I've needed.

"What about you, Dorian?" I finally open my eyes and find his in the mirror. My heart pangs at how good it looks to have him wrapped around me so possessively. "How many times have you called out my name while you fucked your hand?"

Chapter 9

A smirk tilts one side of his mouth right before he buries two fingers inside of me. "Every single one."

My head falls back on his shoulder, the mix of his words and the fullness of his thick fingers stealing my ability to keep it up. Too many times, I've considered what it would be like to finish what we started that night. To see if my imagination was close to what the real thing is like.

It didn't even hold a candle to it.

"You're fucking drenched, Evelyn," he whispers into my neck as he curls his fingers, hitting spots that already have me seeing stars. "Maybe I should be a gentleman and lick you clean before I make you even messier."

He draws his digits halfway out but stops when I whimper in protest. He lets out a little huff before continuing to draw out.

My eyes snap open, and I put on the most serious face I can muster in my current situation. "Dorian, if you move your hand another fucking inch, I swear to God, I'm donkey-kicking you."

His hand flexes around my throat, a wicked grin spreading across his face. "Let's get one thing straight right now, E." He slides his fingers back inside, pressing the heel of his palm against my throbbing clit. "Tonight, you're nothing but my little toy."

He trails soft kisses along my shoulder as his fingers start fucking me in earnest. "You're mine to play with however I fucking please."

Why does that send a new rush of blood coursing to my pussy?

He presses his hand down harder, rocking my clit with even more force as his digits continue their assault.

"You'll do everything I say when I say it."

He picks up his pace, twisting his fingers so quickly, a glint of light flashes behind my eyes.

66

"You'll breathe when I want you to."

Dorian's grip on the sides of my throat has slowly strengthened, and it's only now that I'm realizing how hard it is to take a full breath. It makes my entire body tremble, need surging through me so fast, I'm dizzy.

"You'll come when I tell you to."

The hand on my neck moves me, forcing me to peel my eyes open. Somehow, without me realizing it, we've gotten closer to the mirror. My skin is flushed, my impending orgasm mere seconds away, and the pure hunger in my eyes is enough to tell him how every word is singing straight to my libido.

"And you're going to be a good fucking girl and take everything I give you."

I think I nod, but I'm not sure. Light erupts in my head, and I combust around my best friend's brother's hand. The orgasm rips through my limbs, the built-up teasing beforehand only strengthening how hard I convulse around his fingers.

His lips find the shell of my ear, and he nips at the lobe. "Squeeze your cunt, sunshine."

I start to open my mouth, but then he bites harder. "*Now.*"

I do what I'm told, squeezing against the contractions. The sensation is foreign to me and somehow heightens everything more. My mouth opens on a wild moan, and I push my hips back, driving my ass into him harder.

"You feel that, Evelyn? That sweet pussy of yours wants to give me another one," he purrs in my ear before gliding his tongue up the column of my neck. "Be a sweet girl and give it to me."

He starts to move his fingers all over again, driving them inside of me harder, somehow both extending my orgasm and building up another. The sensation is overwhelming, lighting my body from the inside out as it chases a second high.

I shake my head, a wave of pleasure washing over me again

and again. I feel as though I'm about to be ripped under the tide and dragged underneath. But I can't stop it. I don't *want* to stop it.

My breath stills, the pressure in my core growing with every thrust and twist of his hand. Then, just as it begins to expand, my body quivers, telling Dorian everything he needs to know.

"Atta girl. Let me have it."

The moment the feeling takes over, a loud roll of thunder and crack of lightning vibrates the walls. This orgasm is somehow stronger than the first, rushing through me until I'm panting for air and leaning against him for support.

My entire body goes lax in his arms, forcing him to slide his hand from my neck to wrap around my waist to hold me up. He slips his fingers from my pussy, making me wince slightly. "You did so damn good, sunshine."

Any real words to describe what I'm feeling evade me, but I blow out a shaky breath and whisper, "Holy shit, Dorian. I can't believe we just—I just..."

I feel him smile against my neck. "Yeah, about fucking time. That was a nice little warm-up to get us started."

"Warm up?" I try to turn in his arms, but he holds me steady.

"In what world would two be considered an acceptable number, E?"

My eyes widen as I take in his extremely serious expression in the reflection of the mirror. "I-um—"

I don't get to finish that thought, because the sound of heels echoing up the stairwell cuts me short.

He finally releases me, dropping his hand from my waist to my hand—a notion that feels strangely normal—and ushers us out the door.

Dorian

CHAPTER TEN

Clue 17: The killer is over six feet tall, but it's unclear if they are wearing heels or not.

I reread the simple sentence over a dozen times before handing it to Evelyn with the other evidence we found in the envelope. We've moved into the next room, which just so happens to be the dining area, and it's taking all of my self-control not to throw her against the credenza and start all over again.

But I want to give her a breather. I know she's completely fine after two orgasms, but it's not that I'm worried about. It's about who I am—or who I have been—up until five minutes ago.

I've always had feelings for her. Always knew she could easily be it for me. But in my effort to do what I thought was right, I built a wall filled with spiders and sharp bricks. Now that I've ripped it down in a matter of seconds, I'm trying to tread lightly.

Nevertheless, the urge to rip the dress from her body and completely devour her is getting harder to ignore. All I can think of is the way she squeezed around my fingers, how her lips parted, and her entire body flushed pink from her arousal.

I shuffle forward on the balls of my feet before hooking a finger in her tiny apron and drawing her closer to me. "E."

She reads over the clue again before glancing up at me through her thick lashes, feigning complete indifference. "What?"

An odd sort of trepidation drips down my spine. I've never been nervous before. Not in my adult life, that is, and definitely not around a woman I just finger fucked. But still, it's Evelyn.

Even saying her damn name makes my heart beat a little faster.

"What are you thinking about?"

She blinks, clearly surprised by my question, but quickly masks it. "I'm thinking that it would be extremely ironic if you were the killer."

This makes me chuckle. "It would fit, though."

She cracks a smile, and my heart melts. "It would. But honestly..." She trails off, her eyes drifting to nothing in particular. "I'm still kind of reeling from what just happened."

I release her apron and move my knuckle under her chin, tilting her face up to look at me. "Are you okay?"

Her cheeks bloom that pretty pink, and if I weren't so concerned with what she's thinking, I'd kiss her. I've wondered for a long time what her lips would feel like against mine.

Eve nods, her gaze drifting down to my mouth. "Yeah. I'm trying not to seem—"

Her voice cuts off as I drag my tongue over my bottom lip, understanding washing over me. "Needy?"

She lets out the smallest whimper, and it yanks at the thin piece of thread holding my self-control in place.

"What are your limits, Evelyn?"

She swallows around my words, her eyes still stuck on my lips. "I don't know. I've never tested them."

Why that causes a flare of satisfaction to bloom in my chest is beyond me, but I don't even care. I want to have so many of her firsts that nothing after me will be enough. I want to ingrain myself in every part of her, so she's ruined for any other man.

"Are any places off-limits?"

She shakes her head, her voice barely above a whisper. "No."

I shift my hand to stroke the side of her jaw, loving the way she leans into my touch. We've never had the opportunity to be soft with one another, and now, it's all I want to do.

Too bad this is probably for one night only.

I know her. She'll allow herself this one time to get everything out and then pretend it never happened. My heart squeezes at the thought.

Guess I'll have to leave her sore enough to remind her who owned every inch of her until she comes to her senses.

"Would you like to come again, sunshine?" My voice comes out low and husky, and her body's visceral response is almost more than I can handle.

"Yes," she breathes.

I smirk, dropping my hand from her face and grabbing either side of her hips. Leaning forward, I let my mouth brush against the shell of her ear, reveling in the tiny shivers that rack through her body. "Turn off the light and come right back."

I back away slowly, allowing her a second to do as told. The dining area is partially secluded, and from where everyone is currently supposed to be, the only chance of someone walking in on us is my sister. With the light off, and the way I plan to make her come, it's only barely treading the line of exhibitionism.

Looking over the table briefly, I sit in the best seat and wait as Eve flips off the light, shrouding herself in the dark. A small amount of light peeks in from the kitchen and foyer behind her, giving me a beautiful outline of her figure as she returns to me.

"Sit," I tell her, reaching up and toying with the tip of her fingers.

She uses them as guides until she's straddled on top of me, her lace-covered pussy directly on top of my dick. "Who would have thought I could be both terrified and turned on by being with you in the dark?"

This makes me chuckle. "Be honest. You've always known."

Even though I can't make out her features in the dark, I can feel her roll her eyes. Again, I have to bite back my desire to kiss her but allow myself to get close, brushing my lips along hers just enough to make her squirm over my erection.

Too many times, I've imagined us here, but to finally have it, to know there's a chance at something I've wanted for so long... My heart swells and squeezes in tandem, hope spreading through me faster than I can try to stop it.

"Tell me what you want," I whisper.

She doesn't hesitate. "You."

"*Where* do you want me?" I grip one side of her hips, holding her steady, while my free hand glides up her stomach to the tops of her breasts.

She pushes her chest closer, letting out a small groan. "Everywhere, Dorian."

"Hmm." I push her back slightly before tugging her frilly top down, freeing her breasts.

Her moans grow louder, and I pinch a nipple hard, earning me a squeak of surprise. "Quiet, or this will be over too soon, E."

She's silent for a moment before she lets out a begrudging, "Fine."

This makes me smile. I like this side of her grumpiness. "Before we start, we need a word if I ever push too far. If you find yourself overwhelmed, past what's comfortable."

"Spider." She catches me off guard with how fast she says it.

"Spider?"

Eve nods. "Sounds appropriate since I hate them."

I grin, pressing a soft kiss on her nose. "Spider it is. Also, I need to confess something."

Her eyes narrow in question while my heart begins thrumming into my sternum. I don't know why my nerves are suddenly tight at the thought of my admission, but my stomach twists as I kiss her nose again. "I'm clean. I haven't slept with anyone since Valentine's when you stayed over, and made me and C watch those movies with you. You'd made a comment about how romantic it was when the man is head over heels, and it stuck."

Her pupils flare, a light blush creeping across her cheeks. "Oh."

I drag my lip through my teeth. "Yeah."

"I am, too. Clean, I mean, and on birth control."

I smile at the way her sentences come out. I think I like embarrassed E, too. There's a sort of charm to it in contrast to her ever-present confidence. "Good to know. Now, I need you to stay very still."

Whether she realizes it or not, she's been constantly shifting on top of my lap, her greedy little cunt chasing the friction from my erection pressing into her center. While it feels fucking amazing and has my cock aching to be inside of her, I need her completely still for what I have planned next.

Out of nothing but defiance, she readjusts herself, sliding over the length of my dick before settling on top. "Ready."

I make a note to punish her for that later, but being that this is our first time, I have to keep everything as gentle as I physically can. Which is harder for me than I'd like to admit.

Slowly, I snake a hand behind her, holding her spine steady as I lean forward. My free hand traces over her breasts with featherlight pressure, over and across, down and under.

Small little whimpers flow from her lips, one after the other, and if I wasn't so dead set on how I want to make her come, I'd probably have already given in to her cries and let her grind one out on my lap.

"Patience, sunshine," I whisper against her flesh before dragging my tongue through the valley of her breasts.

Fuck. She's so goddamn soft. Every part of her. I want to explore every single inch and crevice until I've memorized it all. I want to know which nerves make her shake when I pass over them. Which ones make her cry out or the ones that make her shiver. There's no part of her I want to leave unchecked by my hand, and if I have it my way, there won't be a single inch of her I haven't kissed.

That I haven't marked.

I take one nipple into my mouth while I pinch the other in tandem. I suck, bite, tug, and twist, changing how much pressure I apply based on her reaction. Twice, I have to tighten my hand around her back in a silent warning to stay still. But like everything else, I really enjoy her not being able to control her own body.

I love her reactions. Her need. It sends my blood pulsing through me so quickly I'm almost certain if she *did* move, I'd come. No one has ever had such a strong effect on me.

No one but her.

Moving to the other breast, I repeat the process, stimulating the rock-hard little buds until I feel her start to shake. Anyone who's come from nipple play alone knows how surprisingly intense it can be. The erogenous zone is one of many, and if given the right amount of attention by the right person, it can lead to—

"*Dorian.*" She cries my name as she comes, and I swear to God, it's the most beautiful sound I've ever heard.

Her thighs tense around me with every contraction of her cunt, and on the third time she squeezes, I drop my hands to grab her hips, jerking her forward.

She latches on to my shoulders in an attempt to steady herself from the sudden shift, but as soon as I thrust my hips up and make contact with her swollen clit, she melts into me.

"I want you to come again, sunshine."

She leans forward, resting her forehead against mine, her breath coming out in small pants. "I can't, Dorian."

I shake my head, grinding upward. "Yes, you can, Evelyn."

It only takes a few hard movements before she works herself up into a frenzy, rolling her hips to meet mine. I continue my assault on the tender flesh of her nipples but am careful not to push too hard, hence why I have *her* riding my lap, chasing another orgasm.

She's already going from barely getting one to what I hope will be about ten in one night, and it would be irresponsible as fuck to push her any more than that.

I want to get her addicted first. Then, maybe I can break her.

Her fingers dig into my shoulders as she grinds down, her legs trembling as she starts to peak.

"That's it, E. Use me." I grip her harder, hissing as her nails pierce into my shoulders. "Don't you fucking stop."

In the next shift, she grabs one of my hands and brings it to her mouth, biting into the side as she screams through another orgasm. My own blood soars, my dick becoming painfully engorged at her every motion. There's only one thing I want more than to be inside of her, and it's to hear her come again.

75

I continue to move for her when she begins to shake, unable to do it herself with the wave of shudders coursing through her. When her shivers finally begin to subside, I run my hand up and down her spine, whispering soft praises into her hair. "You did so well, sunshine."

She hums a response, her body pressing against mine as her muscles relax. "Yeah?"

I nod, hooking my finger under her chin again so she can see me. "The fucking best, E."

I can barely see it, but the faint smile spreading across her face is enough to make a man fall to his knees, and I can't stop myself from kissing her. Not anymore.

Unlike what I've always imagined, it's soft and sensual. It's filled with all the times I've wanted to tell her how beautiful she was instead of jumping at her from around a corner. The thousands of times I had to stop myself from tapping her nose when she said some of the cutest shit. For every day I've wanted to kiss her, tell her how much I cared about her.

I say it all with my lips, praying that she understands some of it.

Thunder rolls through the building, indicating the few seconds we have left until another pair walks in.

"I need to take you somewhere."

I lift her up, right her skirt, adjust her top, and run a hand through her hair. When I turn on the light, I see her chest is still heaving, her cheeks a dusty pink, eyes wide, and never have I seen someone so breathtakingly gorgeous.

"But the game. We have to go to the next room, or your sister is gonna have a tantrum."

I shake my head, threading my fingers through hers and tugging her to follow me. "Fuck the game for a minute, E. I need my mouth on that cunt."

Evelyn

CHAPTER ELEVEN

I'm ninety percent sure I won't be able to come back from this—whatever *this* is—and no amount of wishing it away will do anything to make me forget what's happening.

It isn't *just* what we're doing. It's all the unsaid things that are starting to surface. It's the way when he touches me, my body somehow feels like it's on fire but relaxed to a degree I've never experienced before. It's when he looks at me, like there's nothing more important he'd rather have his attention on.

When he kissed me... it was like I was *his*.

He isn't the wildcard I thought he was, and, on the contrary, I've never felt safer.

There's something so much deeper happening than the physical part of what we're doing, and I'd be lying if I said I wasn't terrified of what comes after.

With my hand still firmly in his, Dorian pushes open the wide double doors to the game room. Inside, there are two long leather couches, a corner bar, an en suite bathroom, and a pool table. The lighting is low, the only source coming from the three pendant light hanging over the table.

I vaguely remember how the pictures online showcased it as where the groom's party gets ready for the ceremony.

Chapter 11

Dorian finally drops my hand to close the doors, and the sudden absence of his touch leaves a heaviness over my chest I can't quite place.

When he turns to face me, my eyes immediately drop to the dark spot over his groin. I feel my face flame. "Oh—I'm—"

Dorian's head tilts to the side in question, but when he follows my line of sight to the evidence of my arousal, the widest smile stretches across his face.

"I'm sorry."

"Why? It's proof of a job well done, if you ask me. Now," he gestures behind me with his chin, "on the table."

My mouth parts to be a smartass and say something funny, but when he lifts his eyebrows in warning, I can't help but oblige.

What can I say? He's kind of sexy when he orders me around.

Still, I huff my faux annoyance as I twirl, sauntering a little too slowly to the table.

"Are you always going to give me attitude when I give you an instruction?"

I shrug, placing the flat of my hand on the table and jumping, hoisting myself up and turning to face him. "Are you saying there'll be more occasions where you tell me what to do?"

My tone implies I'm being a little sarcastic, but the underlying seriousness is there. I need to know if he feels it too, or if, for him, this is exactly the hate-fuck he said it was.

He takes a slow step forward, folding his sleeves up one at a time. "If I had it my way, sunshine, you'd belong to me after this."

My heart and core clench in unison, butterflies breaking free from their dusty cages. My entire insides are buzzing, vindication seeping into my bloodstream.

Running my tongue over my top teeth to hide a smile, I tilt my head. "Oh yeah?"

Dorian gives me a curt nod. "Yep."

"And why..." I trail off for a moment, spreading my legs open and putting my hands between them to grip the front of the table. "Do you think you deserve to have me after all your petty little games?"

He huffs, dragging his thumb under his lip as his eyes fall to my hands. I wriggle my fingers and kick my legs, hoping the air of nonchalance fools him.

I know him too well, though. I'm more than positive he can see how fast my pulse is thrumming from the vein in my neck. How quick my chest is rising from my quickened breath. I want exactly what he's offering, and he knows it.

"How about this? After we leave here, I give that cunt of yours a break." He steps closer, gripping both of my knees. His calloused fingers feel so good against my skin, and my willpower to seem unfazed by his touch dwindles.

My eyelids flutter closed as he tightens his hold. "We can go room to room for a little bit, play Ciara's game."

I suck in a sharp breath, jerking upright as he shoves my knees apart, pushing his body between my thighs.

"And if I find out who the killer is first, you agree to entertain whatever this is." His voice is so low and husky, my clit starts to throb all over again.

"And if I figure it out first?"

He shoots me a wink before pushing me down flat on my back. "You won't. I want you too bad."

His words act as shots of dopamine to my heart, spreading through me with each pump. Who would've fucking thought this man had the ability to make me swoon?

Dorian's hand trails up my thigh, and my skin responds immediately, sprouting goose bumps under his touch. His fingers reach the lace covering my pussy, and he tugs, slipping them from my body in one smooth motion.

I try to sit up on my elbows to see him, but when he stands, straightening his spine to tower over me, I lay back down. I like the feeling of having him like this. At one point, it would have scared the shit out of me, but now, it makes my entire body sing.

My legs are still spread wide open, baring myself to him, naked in the most intimate way. Some part of me is sure I'm supposed to be uncomfortable, but the look of pure hunger etched into his sharp features makes me feel like a five-course meal.

"Do you know how fucking stunning you look right now?"

I bite into my lip, anticipation dripping over me with his words.

He swipes a finger through my slit, making me jolt, before sliding it into his mouth. A guttural groan vibrates from his chest as he licks it clean. "How good you taste?"

Holy shit, that's hot.

"Once I start, I'm not stopping unless you say your word. Do you understand?"

I swallow around the sudden lump in my throat. I'm nervous. Why am I suddenly nervous?

He taps my thigh, garnering my attention as he lowers to his knees. "Words, baby. They're important."

A shiver flutters through me, and I have to fight to find the remnants of my voice. "Yes."

"That's my girl."

With that, he dips between my thighs and licks me from entrance to clit.

My eyes roll back, a feeble whimper falling freely from my mouth as jolts of pleasure shoot through me. His fingers grip my thighs, holding me steady as he laves at my clit.

I want to stay still, to resist the urge to chase his face, but the way he's working me, I can't help it. Reaching down, I run my fingers through the short patch of rough curls on the top of his head and pull him closer.

Somehow, someway, I want more.

I *need* it.

He chuckles against my sensitive skin before jerking me to the edge of the table, lifting my ass higher. He tilts my body upward, forcing me to wrap my legs around his shoulders.

My heel presses into his back in an attempt to keep me steady, but then he sucks my clit in his mouth, and I can no longer move. I'm stuck in place. At his complete mercy to do whatever the hell he sees fit.

The pressure is already building too quickly, and I've never had to battle wanting something but also not at the same time.

"Dorian, I'm too close."

"Hmm." He draws back slightly, replacing his mouth with his fingers, and rubs steady circles over my clit. "You want to prolong it?"

My lips part twice before I can form a simple phrase. "I don't know. I want to come, but it feels so good I don't want you to stop."

"What a tangled web we weave."

I roll my eyes. "Okay, Sir Scott."

Dorian's brows furrow, and his hand pauses. "That wasn't Shakespeare?"

"*Dorian.*"

He huffs out a laugh, resuming his hand's movement between my thighs. "I've decided I want something else before the night is over."

I'm not able to respond this time because he slips his finger inside of me, curling in a torturous way as he lowers himself back into place. He drags his tongue up my pussy before sucking my throbbing clit in his mouth again. "I want to hear what you sound like when you beg for me."

His words spur the pressure to build all over again, and it only takes a few more times of him combining the lick, suck, and curl of digits before I explode, coming shamelessly on his tongue.

The sensations ripple through me yet again, threatening to tear me apart. This time, it feels as though my whole body is pulsing in tandem with my cunt, clenching and releasing with every wave.

He continues to fuck me with his tongue until I'm damn near panting and shivering around him. "*Dorian.*"

"Hmm." He doesn't move but slows down, easing his movements until my body stops tensing.

Shit. There's no way in hell I can live the rest of my life without feeling his mouth on me again.

"Up." Dorian grips my hips and helps me rise slowly.

It's only now I'm starting to realize how much energy is being sucked out of me each time I come. My muscles tremble as he helps steady me on my feet, running an idle hand down my spine.

"I need to know if you're okay or if we need to take a break."

I chew on my bottom lip, savoring the sweet Dorian that's eluded me until now. This is the guy everyone used to say was the sweetest thing they ever met. The one who does anything to help a complete stranger.

Part of me is glad I never saw this side of him before. It makes the moment all the more tender. "I'm fine. More than fine. I'm perfect."

He narrows his eyes, but when I lift on my tiptoes and whisper, "One more," against his lips, his entire body goes rigid.

His grip on my hips tightens, and he turns me roughly, pressing into my back and forcing me to bend over the pool table. I let out a playful squeal as he lifts my skirt, tossing it over my waist.

"I really want to take my time with this part, but I have less than five minutes till that damn thunder goes off."

"And you think you can get me off that quick?" My tone is borderline cocky as I turn my face to the side, watching in my periphery as he draws his chain out from the inside of his shirt.

On the end, there's a small cylinder shaped like a thin lipstick vial. He tugs on the chain, popping the bottom off and tipping the contents into his hand.

"What is that?" I arch my back, interest piqued as he recaps the empty shell.

He drops his hand to the top of my ass, rubbing in small circles. Completely bypassing my question, he trails his fingers down, stopping when he reaches my tight ring of muscle. "Have you ever been touched here?"

I suck in a sharp breath. "No."

If I weren't staring so intently, I'd probably miss the tic in his jaw. "What a fucking waste."

He shakes his head and continues his perusal of my ass until his hand reaches my right knee. He lifts it up, hoisting it on top of the pool table and spreading me apart. The cool air causes a shiver to rack through me, making Dorian chuckle.

"I'll never get tired of your responses to me." With that, he taps the top of the gold cylinder, and it whirls to life.

It's a fucking vibrator.

"I got this to use on you so long ago, and for a while, I didn't think I'd ever get to." He presses the small bullet to the outside of my slit, and I nearly jump out of my skin, scooting away from him on reflex.

How the hell is that little thing so strong?

83

Chapter 11

Dorian flexes his hand at the small of my back, his voice dropping an octave. "Never fucking run from me, sunshine. Not unless you want me to chase you."

His double innuendo speaks to a fantasy I've never dared to utter out loud, and I must make a face, because Dorian calls it out immediately.

"Hmm. Don't tell me you've thought about me chasing you before, E. I don't think my cock could handle it."

I moan as he moves the vibrator, shifting it closer to where I need it.

"You like it when I jump out at you? When I used to chase you around the house?"

I try to shake my head, but he places the toy right on top of my clit, holding it there for a brief second before taking it away.

"*Dorian*," I hiss through clenched teeth, thrusting my hips backward. "We don't have much time."

He lets out a low chuckle, allowing me a moment's relief with the vibrator, then snatching it away. He does it three more times till I'm whimpering with need.

"Please, Dorian." I hate how desperate my voice sounds, but right now, I can't find it in me to care.

I can hear the smile in his voice. "Tell me what I want to know, and I'll put it back."

I blow out a large breath of frustration, my muscles tightening with the on and off of his touch. "You want to know if I've ever imagined you chasing me and fucking me in the mask from that night? Maybe once or twice. Happy now?"

He stills behind me. The moment is no longer than a second, but it feels like an eternity. Right as I start to peek over my shoulder, he presses the toy directly against my clit, leaving it there until I'm scratching and clawing at the table beneath me.

My next two orgasms slam into me back to back, leaving me

a trembling mess hanging on for what feels like my life. But even as I'm shaking, wondering how I'm going to walk in my six-inch heels after this, Dorian wraps his arms around my waist and tells me how incredible I'm doing. How proud he is of me.

His heavy hand strokes over my hair as he leads me to the en suite. "Let's get you cleaned up, sunshine."

Evelyn

CHAPTER TWELVE

After cleaning me up and washing his hands, he somehow convinced me I needed a break. He claims too much, too soon can be dangerous, and I need to listen to my body.

Well, my body is fucking exhausted, but I've never craved a man inside me so bad in my life.

He laughed when I said that and told me we still had a game to play. I had to bite my tongue from telling him that no matter who wins, this isn't ending tonight. There's no way in hell I'm not going to be warming his bed for at least the next week—after my sore cunt gets some R and R, of course.

"Did you write it down?" Dorian holds his hand out for the new clue we found in the sunroom.

It's the third room since we left the game room, which means, if I do a quick math calculation, it's been forty-five minutes of my pussy going untouched by this man.

"Yes." My words come out a little curt, but I'm quick to apologize. "Sorry. I did, thank you."

He smirks as he takes it from me, sliding it back into the envelope and tucking it in its hiding place. "You alright?"

I nod. "Just peachy."

He hooks his index finger under my jaw and tilts my face up so he can look into my eyes. "You want me to fuck you?"

I nod again. "Yes, please."

He laughs at this, and the low sound travels straight to my core, making me squeeze my thighs together. "If I would've known you'd be so damn sweet from a few orgasms, I would have done this a long time ago."

"Fuck off, Dorian." I roll my eyes and stand, glancing over my clue sheet. "When I win, I'm making *you* beg for it."

"I'll do that now if you want. I'll drop to my knees and worship every last inch of you until you let me have my fill. No winning necessary."

My mouth parts, the desire to accept his offer so strong, I almost don't hear the crash of lightning signaling our transition. It isn't until Sir Saffron and his partner open the door that I realize we need to move.

Dorian loops his arm around my waist, drawing me into his side as we pass the pair. I wait until we're in the foyer before I shimmy out of his hold and smirk. "Jealous?"

He doesn't hesitate to answer. "Absolutely."

His answer takes me by surprise, and my head jolts back. "I definitely wasn't expecting that."

Dorian shrugs. "As bad as I want to claim it, you're not mine, so I'm jealous of any man who gets your attention."

Not mine. I repeat the phrase a few times in my head before I drag my teeth over my bottom lip. "Is that something you want? For me to be yours?"

His heavy hands find either side of my hips and pull me into his chest. "Sunshine, I've wanted that for longer than I'll ever admit."

He leans in, brushing a soft kiss over my nose before tapping it. "Also, I already know who the killer is. So I guess technically, I get you all to myself for a little bit."

"Wait, what?"

I look down at the white paper in his fist and notice way more markings on it than what I have on mine. Goddamn hormones. I was so caught up in my head, thinking about the next time he would touch me, that I didn't take half as many notes.

I glance over my own paper and try to come up with some type of answer. It's not that I don't want him to win, it's just the competitive side of me would also like to claim the victory of knowing at the same time he does.

"Give me thirty seconds."

He nods. "Sure."

I narrow my eyes at his overly confident *sure* and study my less-than-ideal clue sheet.

> -Has to be a man or a ~~really tall woman~~. No female guest is over 6 feet, even in heels
> -was one of the first guests to arrive. (~~Lavender,~~ Butler, ~~Maid,~~ Saffron, Pea, Crueleon, ~~Magenta,~~ Seafoam.)
> -Right-handed? (dumbest clue ever)
> -A black tie left near crime scene, traces of victim's blood.
> -Drops of Chicken and Gnocchi broth lead away from the body.

In almost any circumstance, I'd be afraid I didn't have enough written down. That I was so worried about Dorian, I let him steal the victory out from under my nose. But this isn't just any circumstance, and it's my attention to him that makes the limited puzzle pieces I have click into place.

Everyone listed as a potential suspect is at or over six feet tall. All of them arrived around the same time, making them the early birds of the group.

Seafoam is left-handed—I noticed when he accepted his pasta dish from me—and Cruelon is wearing a white tie, leaving only Dorian, the butler, and Sir Saffron.

There are two reasons why I know it can't be Saffron. One, a black tie would look hideous with his color combo, not to mention Dorian's went missing shortly after the lights flickered off.

Second, I distinctly remember spilling soup near Dorian's shoe when we were in the kitchen. It's not unreasonable to think he might have stepped in it at one point.

My heart hammers in my chest, and the hairs on the back of my neck rise as I look up from the paper and at the killer who's been fucking me into delirium all night.

"It's you," I whisper, taking a step back. "You murdered Detective Danube."

Dorian smirks, erasing the space I just made between us. "Clever girl."

I shudder at his words, a whole new type of adrenaline leaking into my bloodstream.

"How about I give you a ten-second head start? I think Ciara said she'll be in the maze, waiting for the winner."

I swallow around the lump in my throat as I take another step back. "Ten seconds isn't enough."

Dorian lifts one shoulder, tucking his chain into his shirt. "Then I guess you better get running."

Without another thought, I slip my heels off and sprint down the wide hallway leading outside to the maze. Blood whooshes through my ears as my feet pound into the marble, bites of pain shooting up my spine every time my soles connect with the hard floor.

But I don't stop. I book it at full speed, only slowing down when I reach the door and jerk it open. I don't bother closing it, nor do I look behind me. That's how every victim gets caught in the movies.

They look back once, and they fall. Every. Single. Time.

The cool October air feels refreshing on my suddenly clammy skin, but it's the only good thing about being outside, in the dark, surrounded by hedges I can't see over, with a killer chasing me.

Luckily, Ciara had Dorian set up a recognizable path to the center of the maze, so I don't have to worry about getting lost. Though it *also* means Dorian won't have to search for me.

Panic and trepidation trickle down my temple with the sweat that's formed along my brow. I keep going, my breath quickening as I pass spider webs and their oversized spiders.

My heart thunders in my chest, every pulse harder than the last. What makes it worse is I don't hear him I only hear the sounds of my feet pounding into the ground and my sharp intakes of air.

Even though I can't hear him, I can't bring myself to look. I know as soon as I do, he'll be there.

Still...

Nope. Don't be the token character in the movies.

I keep going, knowing the center has to be coming up.

Then I hear it.

"I may have lied."

It's Dorian. I can't pinpoint exactly where his voice is, but it's not behind me.

"It's just you and me out here, E."

Fucking hell.

Of course, I fell for that. Why in the world would Ciara be out here when she's got disgruntled employees in the house? Shit. He's most likely already in the center. He must know a shortcut.

I consider turning around, but I worry he might have locked the damn door.

Shit. Shit. Shit.

Fuck it. I veer off one of the adjacent paths and run. I don't know where the hell I'm going, but if I come out on the other side, I can round the property and get to the front door.

Adrenaline pushes my feet harder into the ground. Hues of green become blurry as I run past them, turning left and right, then right again.

My legs feel as though they're two seconds away from becoming mush, but I keep going. I'm at least seventy percent sure I see some type of opening ahead.

I use my last bit of energy to propel myself forward, and as soon as I break through said opening, I'm captured around the waist.

My shrill scream pierces through the air as I'm slung around, falling with Dorian. He hits the ground first, landing on his back while he cradles me on top.

"Got you."

I try to push out of his hold, bucking and wriggling against him, but instead of the expected alarm or pure dread, something else blooms in my core. We're both panting, our limbs fighting one another as we try to do the opposite of the other.

Finally, as if he's a lion done toying with his food, he grabs both of my wrists and flips me over effortlessly, coming down on top of me. His harsh breaths blow the hair from my face, while my chest heaves, arousal taking over every inch of my body.

Dorian's dark eyes rove over me, taking in every minute detail of my face. Somehow, he looks even hungrier than he has all night, and for the first time, fear trickles into my bloodstream. It's a delicious feeling, and it turns out, *I like it.*

"Do you still want me to fuck you, sunshine?"

My cheeks flush pink as I nod. "Yes."

"Here?"

I nod again. "I can't wait."

Dorian's jaw tenses before he runs his tongue along his bottom lip. "One time, Evelyn. Then I'm taking you home, and I'm going to fuck you on every surface of your house so there isn't a place you can look where you haven't come on my cock."

With that, he crashes his lips against mine. Unlike the first time, this is with an intensity I've never felt before. It's as though years of desire, annoyance, need, and missed chances are put into every part of it. As if he needs me to know just how long he's waited for this moment and doesn't want to waste a single second.

A violent tremor racks through me at his promise, the ones both said and unspoken. My voice comes out a mere whisper. "Please."

In the next breath, Dorian's jacket is on the ground and my skirt is thrown up around my waist. He undoes his belt but moves so slowly that I start to squirm with impatience. "*Dorian.*"

He smirks, the arrogant side of him I've come to know making an appearance. When he finally glides his zipper down and releases his erection from his briefs, I actually gasp. It all makes sense, and I realize why he has every reason in the world to be a cocky asshole.

I shake my head. "There's no way I can take that more than once, Dorian."

He chuckles, grabbing my hips and hoisting me up at an angle that allows me to watch when he enters. "Baby, not only will you take it, you'll beg me for it."

He runs the head of his dick through my slit, both coating it in my arousal and making me writhe beneath him. A few more passes and I realize it could be the size of King Kong, and I wouldn't care, I want him inside of me.

"*Dorian.*"

"Remember your word?" He lines himself up with my entrance, pushing the head in just enough to make me hiss.

I nod. "Yes."

"Good."

Then, just as I think he's about to drive inside of me, he slips a small ball of fabric from his pocket.

My panties.

He'd taken them when we were cleaning up from the pool table.

He taps my lip with his index finger. "Open."

I furrow my brows, natural defiance seeping out, even in my wanton state. "I don't need those. Plus, they're probably soaked."

He taps my lip again. "One, you taste so fucking good, I know it'll turn you on. Second, not to be presumptuous, but you're gonna scream, E."

I narrow my eyes but do as he commands because if he's not inside of me in the next two seconds, I *will* be screaming. "Fine."

Gently, he places the fabric in my mouth, and fuck if it isn't the sexiest and dirtiest thing I've ever experienced. It makes me acutely aware that we're outside, on the ground, in the middle of a party, where anyone can walk out on us.

The taste of the fabric and remnants of my arousal only push that feeling into overdrive, and I tilt my hips up in a silent plea.

He smirks, gliding his hands down my side before grabbing either side of my hips.

Then, without another warning, he tears me in half.

Dorian

CHAPTER THIRTEEN

For the first time in my life, I know I'm not gonna last.

Evelyn's cunt is too hot and too fucking wet for me to confidently say I can make her come at least three times before I do. Which is a fucking crime already, if you ask me.

I mean, I knew she'd feel good, but pair that with her reactions? I'm a goner.

To buy myself a little time and give her some to adjust to my size, I rub small circles over her hip bone with my thumb. "How we doing down there?"

With the panties in her mouth, she simply gives me a thumbs-up.

"Can I slide in more?"

Her eyes flare, and I clearly understand her muffled, "More?"

"There's a lot left."

Her face blooms that delicious pink as she nods, and I decide to do us both a small act of mercy and drive all the way inside her.

My groan matches her wild moans as her pussy stretches to

accommodate me. Even though I know it's an adjustment for her, I swear she's a perfect fit.

Everything about her and how we are together only proves the notion I've had all along. She's mine. Made for me and only me, and there won't be another day that passes that she doesn't know it.

I draw out and slide back in, hating how heat is already trying to lick its way up my spine. "This pretty little cunt was made for me. You know that, sunshine?"

Again, I pull out and glide in, keeping my pace smooth and steady. "That's why you're taking me so well."

Her moans morph into cries and whimpers as I move, dragging my cock all the way out to the head before burying myself back inside. Her pussy grips around me as I move, squeezing around my dick every time I pause.

She grasps on to my forearms, digging her nails into the muscles, her legs drifting open wider.

"That's it. Open up for me, baby." I hook my arm under her thighs and lift, wrapping them around my waist. "Let's see exactly what you're capable of."

With that, I slam into her over and over again. My strokes are long and hard, unforgiving and brutal. They're filled with every emotion she's ever made me feel, all the times I wanted to do this but couldn't.

For when she stood in front of me, her chest puffed up and her face red as she argued with me about something petty when all I wanted to do was kiss her. When she knowingly walked past me, swaying her hips into my kitchen before snagging one of my drinks.

For every time I wanted to tell her how I feel but didn't.

Her cunt contracts around me, her first orgasm tearing through her. Even with her makeshift gag, her screams are loud, echoing in the dark space surrounding us. I fuck her through it, gripping her tighter as I drive in deeper every time. It isn't until her contractions weaken that I finally relent, tugging the red lace from her mouth.

I unhook her legs from around my waist and draw out slowly, pride filling my chest as I watch her face tighten when she's empty.

"How are you feeling?" I ask, flipping her over onto her hands and knees. Her ass is a beautiful red, small streaks decorating it from where the faux grass dug into her skin.

"I can take it," is the answer she gives me, her eyes low as she peers at me from over her shoulder.

I smirk, threading my fingers through her hair before yanking back, running my tongue along the column of her sweet neck. "Oh, I know you can. But since you're so confident, I want you to fuck yourself with my cock while I sit here and watch."

She lets out a hiss as I tighten my grip on her hair. "I can't come again, Dorian."

I release a chuckle. "Yes, you can. Now, sit the fuck down."

She sucks in a sharp breath but does as told, sitting back on her knees, spreading her legs on either side of mine. It's nothing more than reverse cowgirl, but with me sitting up and her pussy open, it allows my cock to hit different places and frees up room for my hands.

Evelyn sinks down on my dick, and the groan that slips free of my mouth makes her shiver against me.

She places both hands on top of my thighs and starts to grind. It's slow at first as she adjusts to the new position, but once she gets her rhythm, she picks up the pace.

"Atta girl, sunshine. Take what you need. It's yours."

She lets out a moan at my words, her bounces becoming harder and harder as she chases yet another orgasm.

I have to admit, I'm impressed with how well she's doing, and when I tell her as much, she slams down harder. "It's because it's you."

Each word in that sentence sticks to my heart, delivering blow after blow to whatever doubt I might've had about us being something more after this.

This woman is mine. Now and fucking forever.

I reach around, finding her sensitive clit, rubbing it in sharp circles. "This little cunt belongs to me. Do you understand, sunshine? This is it. There will never be anyone else here after this."

She cries a series of *yeses,* spreading her legs wider as the pleasure comes over her. "It's yours."

Those two little words are my undoing, and the heat I've held at bay finally takes over, threatening to consume me. I speed up my pace on her clit, jerking my hips up, taking over with punishing thrusts.

Her hands tighten on my thighs. "I can't—Dorian. It's too much. This—"

I come at the exact moment she does, the sensation shooting through my body and flooding it so violently, it hurts. She screams out, her cum seeping from her cunt, covering my entire lap.

But I don't stop. I don't stop fucking her until we're both spent and our bodies are nothing more than worn muscle and beating hearts.

When I finally do release her, she slumps forward, planting the flat of her palms against the grass. Her shoulders are shaking, and her pussy is leaking a mixture of our cum. A foreign desire passes over me to shove it all back inside her, but instead, I lean forward, rubbing up her back and peppering her spine with soft kisses.

"You did so good, sunshine."

Chapter 13

She lets out a feeble laugh. "I'm pretty sure I'm about to die."

"Then I did my job right," I whisper over her skin before sitting back, pulling my slacks up over my hips. They're drenched from her cum, which means it's time for us to go. "Let's get you home and cleaned up."

"But Ciara. The party." Her voice is nowhere near convincing that she cares about either of those things, but I nod, slipping my phone out and drafting a text to my sister. I'll push send when we're already in the car.

"Let me worry about Ciara. My priority is taking care of you right now. No discussions about it."

I can tell she wants to reject the statement, but after another second of thought, she nods, reaching a hand out and gripping on to me to help her stand. I right her skirt and brush her hair from her face at the same moment she looks down and realizes what's happened.

"Is... is that from me?"

I nod. "Yep."

"I—" She stares down at the mess, her eyes wide.

"Never squirted before either?"

She shakes her head. "No."

I yank her close, turning to walk us back through the maze and toward the estate. "Good."

We make it to the door before I find my sister standing in front of it, one hand on her hip while her eyes scan over a paper in her hand. I try to make a sharp turn and avoid her, but it's too late. She looks up, and her jaw nearly hits the ground when she sees how disheveled we are.

"I *fucking* knew it. I knew that if I just gave y'all a little time, you would finally realize how crazy you are for each other." Ciara's eyes bounce between the two of us, standing hand in hand like it's the most natural thing in the world.

Funny thing is, that's exactly what it feels like.

"Oh, I always knew. I was just waiting for her to catch up." I nudge Evelyn softly with my shoulder before tugging her toward my car. "Great party, sis."

Ciara laughs, shooting me a wink and a wave. "Thank you. But you owe Jamie and me a few drinks since *clearly,* we'll be stuck here, cleaning up."

"Consider us even for you knowing your best friend put cayenne pepper in my boxers and not saying anything. And the fact that you made me the killer." I wave over my shoulder. "Also, I highly doubt Jamie will complain about having some alone time with you."

Her mouth gapes open, and Evelyn giggles beside me as we walk toward the car. "You knew?"

I smirk, throwing my arm around E. "I know a love-sick puppy when I see one."

Eve shakes her head. "You notice everything."

I open her door and usher her inside. "Everything."

Unlike the drive to the estate, when I was thinking about all the ways I was gonna make her pay for putting hot pepper flakes in my boxers, I'm now considering all the ways I want to break her, put her back together, then break her some more.

She hums contentedly the entire ride, and I think it's somewhere between her nose scrunching up about the fact that I secretly like mushroom pineapple pizza and when she laughs about the time I lost Mortal Kombat to her seven times in a row, that I know this woman is truly mine.

When we get home, and I get her through the front door of her place, I tell her exactly that as I carry her up to a much-deserved bath. "You wanna know something?"

She hums, leaning her face into my chest, her eyes already drifting closed.

"You're stuck with me, sunshine."

Chapter 13

Though she appears fully asleep, she grins. "As long as I get the Canadian waters."

A laugh rumbles out of me. "As many as you want."

Evelyn

EPILOGUE

"What number?"

Warm tears streak down my face as I try to somehow catch my breath. "I—it's—"

"You lost count again, sunshine." It's more of a statement than a question, and the notion he thinks there's any way I could possibly forget what number I'm on annoys me immensely.

"Twenty-three," I push out through pursed lips, readjusting my cuffs. The once soft fur now feels like sandpaper scraping against my sensitive wrists.

I squirm. A lot. Because even after a year of being with Dorian Davis, I'll never get used to all the things he makes me feel.

He strokes a rough thumb over my cheek, brushing away the remnants of my latest orgasm. "Can I have one more, baby? Just one."

I can barely think, let alone speak, my body nothing more than raw nerves and a pumping heart, yet somehow, I nod.

I nod.

It's clear at this point that I've lost my mind, but the smile on Dorian's face is enough to make me want to push my limits.

"That's my girl." Dorian tucks a stray hair behind my ear before pressing a soft kiss to my nose. "I'm so proud of you."

Dorian picks up his pace, thrusting inside of me harder now. How in the hell it feels *more* amazing is beyond me, but my head lolls back with the overwhelming sensation. A moan slips out as he drives in and out, moving in ways and hitting spots that have my body clenching tight all over again.

My nerves singe, lightning pulsing through them as it spreads down my limbs. Incoherent murmurs mix with wild moans as my greedy hips lift, meeting each of his harsh strokes.

"I knew you had one more for me." One of his warm hands squeezes my hip, his fingers digging into the tender flesh, while the other reaches above me. The light whirl of my favorite vibrator, the air pulse stimulator, nearly brings tears to my eyes.

He presses it over my swollen clit, and whatever rational thoughts I had left completely vanish.

"Atta girl. Just like that. Don't stop."

I'm not even sure what I'm doing anymore, but I don't stop. I chase the high of my twenty-fourth orgasm that borders the line of pain and pleasure and all things in between. The resounding explosion is crippling. Waves rush through my body like a hurricane, ripping me apart.

Something comparable to a scream tears through my throat, the orgasm threatening to suffocate me. It feels incredible, yet overwhelming, and I can swear I can feel the clench and pulse in the tips of my toes down to the ends of my hair.

It feels as if it goes on forever this time, coming in bursts until I'm straining to catch my breath.

"I got you. Come here."

Somehow, he has me out of the cuffs and curled into his lap just as the throbbing subsides. One of his heavy hands strokes my hair while the other wraps around my back, holding me steady.

"I'm so fucking proud of you, baby," he says against my temple before peppering soft kisses over the spot. "That's the most so far."

I still can't find the words, my brain ninety-five percent pulsing mush, so I simply huff my acknowledgment.

Even though Dorian has expressed wanting to get me to the sixties, he's been patient. He never pushes me past what I'm comfortable with and uses signals I didn't even know I gave to keep me from ever even having to use our safe word.

It's one of the many things I used to despise about him but now love. He reads me as if he wrote my book himself, always finding ways to bring me the most pleasure.

"Breathe with me, E. Deep breaths."

Dorian's chest rises with a deep inhale, and I do my best to match it. It takes almost a dozen before I feel some sort of normalcy in my heart's rhythm.

"How we doing?"

I nod. "Good."

"One to ten?"

I drop my head onto his shoulder and let a soft smile spread across my face. "Eight."

He arches a thick brow. "Oh yeah? Wanna give me another dozen?"

"Oh. See, I'd love to," I chuckle—albeit weakly—and pat a hand against his broad chest. "But can't. We'll be late to Ciara's engagement party."

Dorian shrugs, running a thumb down my jaw. "Jamie will make her forgive us."

I narrow my eyes. He's trying to get me to admit I'm at my limit, but he should know better. I could be three seconds from passing out, and I'd go out talking shit. "It would be incredibly rude if her brother and favorite sister-in-law were late."

"Favorite? More like only."

I wave him off. "Tomato, tomahto. Clean me up so we can go, please."

Dorian smirks, and I'm certain if my pussy wasn't about to fall off, it would be clenching all over again. "Yes, ma'am."

He moves to the end of the bed and stands with me still cradled in his arms. His warmth envelops me as he walks us into our bathroom and sits on the edge of the tub. As always, he runs my bath and nestles in behind me until the residual tremors fade and my body comes back down to earth.

My eyes grow heavy as he takes his time washing my shoulders and arms. Dorian's aftercare can last an hour, and half the time, I'm asleep in the first twenty.

"You getting sleepy on me, sunshine?"

"A little."

He hums. "We have a bit. Take a nap after this."

I shake my head but allow my eyes to close. "You won't wake me in time."

Whenever I decide to listen to him and drift off, he conveniently lets me sleep way past my allotted time. He claims it's because rest is more important than whatever's on my to-do list.

He holds up two fingers in front of me. "Scout's honor."

I roll my eyes. He said the same thing to the officiant when he asked if he promised to have and to hold me through sickness and in health. "Alright. Twenty minutes."

I feel the smirk on his face. "Twenty-four."

Even being madly in love with the man doesn't lessen my desire to sock him in the face, but I guess that's what makes us, us. Nothing has changed in terms of his obsession with making me scream nor my constant readiness to argue him down. Never have I been happier or felt more safe.

This is where I'm supposed to be.

Now and forever, spiders and all.

The End.

Ready for your next kinky holiday read? Pre-Order here.

Coming Valentines '23

Preview of Cupids Peak

Mia

"If you don't get someone to rail you within an inch of your life soon, I'm kicking you out."

My twin sister, Eleni, tosses her phone down on the couch next to me, her lips twisted in a somehow graceful grimace. I've never understood how she's able to do that, but I add it to my mental list of ways she continues to reign supreme in being effortlessly elegant.

"I'm sorry." I pull my pajama-covered legs under me and blow on my hot chocolate, ignoring the soft glow of her phone. "Please explain to me how my having sex has anything to do with my quality as a roommate?"

She brushes her hands over her cream pantsuit. The gorgeous fabric ripples under her touch. "It's like coming home to a sad cat lady with no cats, and it's progressively making your aura suck. You need a good O to bring back some life to those cheeks."

"A good O," I repeat, taking a small sip of my drink and

turning back toward my paused Hallmark movie. "I get those every Friday, thank you."

It's the truth, I really do. In fact, I actually have an assortment of toys—all ordered from a discreet shipping site—and rotate them out every Friday while Eleni's on her dates. I'm what some would call a "shy masturbator," and can't seem to find the spot if I know anyone's around to hear.

Eleni throws her hands up before delicately sitting on the leather accent chair next to our couch. "Orgasms should be spontaneous, Em. Not penciled in like something on an agenda."

"Says the woman who goes on dates every Friday," I counter, raising a defiant brow.

Having a solid schedule is one of the few things my sister and I have in common. Everything else, though? Pretty much the complete opposite.

Where she's assertive, I'm reserved. Where she's Miss Fancy-Pants, I'm Miss Cozy-Sundresses. While she's content in front of a dozen cameras being the spokesperson for a multi-billion-dollar corporation, I'm in the background, working on that same corp's finances from the comfort of my couch.

I've never liked being front and center. There's just too much pressure that comes with people watching you, and even imagining them in their underwear does absolutely nothing to help my fried nerves.

"Em, I go out on Fridays because I'm busy during the week, and my Saturdays belong to friends, while my Sundays are for—"

"Errands, I know," I finish for her, taking another swig from my cat mug. And yes, I see the irony. Both in my cup and her telling me to be spontaneous when she herself lives on a tight schedule. "Again, I'll ask. What do my future pet choices and the origin of orgasms have anything to do with you?"

Eleni sucks her teeth, her dark eyes narrowing. "Because our furniture is too expensive to be scratched to hell, and your cunt needs a little love. It helps with your internal balance."

I wave her off, taking another slow drink. I frown when I notice my whipped cream has already melted. "You're being dramatic, so clearly, there's something brewing. What's up?"

Leaning forward in the chair, my sister crosses her feet at the ankle and rests her hands on her knees. A sly smirk takes over her heart-shaped face. "I got you a date for tonight."

"What?" My brows draw together harshly, the skin pulling taut. "Why the hell would you do that?"

She throws up her hands again. "Because it's Valentine's Day, and you haven't been on a freakin' date in, like, three years."

Annoyance snaps at my rib cage. "Because I've been busting my ass, working close to eighty hours a week."

"Life isn't about working yourself to death, Mia."

"It's not all about having impromptu O's either."

"Then what the hell is it about?" Eleni shakes her head, her dark waves curling around her bronze face. We're both Dominican, but her skin has always been a touch more sun-kissed than mine. *Maybe it's from all her spontaneous orgasms.*

"Look, I'm not asking you to fall in love, but as your sister and best friend, I think you need to live a little, and this is me finally interjecting. Think of it like an intervention or something."

I know my sister's intentions are coming from a good place, and that's the sole reason I don't *accidentally* spill any hot chocolate on her cream pants as I make my way to our kitchen. "And you thought springing this on me the *morning of* would be a great way to do it?"

She snatches her phone from the couch, clearly exasperated that I didn't look at whatever was on the screen. "Of course. It's the only way you'd agree."

That's probably true. Still, I had big plans for today. First, finish my movie, next, stare out of the window at the fresh new layer of snow. Then, maybe take a relaxing bath and watch another movie. It's my day off, so really, the possibilities are limitless. A first date on the love holiday? Definitely not on the agenda.

But also, she's not completely wrong.

My dating life has been, well, for a lack of a better word, dull. The few men I went out with in college weren't looking for anything serious, which I certainly don't blame them for, and the couple after were... not the one.

Hell, now that I think about it, I haven't liked a guy as much as I did this one from my senior year in high school. The funny thing about him was that we never even dated. I'm not even sure if you could define us as real friends. We had random hallway conversations, and then I later tutored him after his math grade threatened to have him benched.

Eli Brooks.

He was the school's *it* guy. Polite, charismatic, with a good sense of humor. A solid trifecta I haven't been able to find since graduating a decade ago. Somewhere in between the late nights and textbooks, I grew really attached to his company. Too bad I couldn't ever muster up my sister's tenacity and tell him.

But even though *we* didn't become something, he did. He's been dubbed the most valuable player on his team in the National Hockey League three years in a row. Not to mention he has somehow become hotter.

Some would say it's a missed opportunity, but I couldn't imagine a worse fate. The man lives in the spotlight. I would have to pop an antacid every twenty minutes.

110

"I promise you'll have a good time. The guy's a gem and can't wait to have dinner."

I inwardly groan as I re-top my hot chocolate with whipped cream. My sister has good taste in men and an even better radar for the keepers—it's how she actively avoids them on her journey of liberation—so I know she means it when she says he's a catch. Still...

"Who is he?" I finally ask, returning to the couch.

A massive smile overtakes her face. "An old friend of mine from school. He's in town for the weekend, and it just so happens my date canceled on me, but I still have reservations up at Cupid's Peak."

So not a date. A one-night stand.

My eyes widen, and I hold up a hand. "Wait. You want me to go on a date with your old buddy to a *five-star* resort under the premise of him being in town for tonight only?"

She sucks her bottom lips in her mouth and scrunches her nose. "Kinda."

"Kinda?"

Eleni stands. "Listen. If you don't want to go, it's nothing for me to cancel with him. I just thought for once that maybe you'd like to step out of that comfort zone of yours and enjoy yourself."

Enjoy myself. I almost laugh at the direct innuendo. But, per usual, she's right. I could use a night out and maybe have a little fun that's not already pre-penciled in. It would be nice. And with everyone paying attention to their date in front of them, there's no worry about them looking at me.

I bounce my answer back and forth in my mind. Best case, I have a good time. Worst case, it's a night free from having to cook or do dishes.

"Fine."

She lets out a little celebratory *eep* before grabbing her coat on the back of the couch. "I'll let him know. I have a brunch date, but when I get back, we're getting you ready!"

Her words have me on the edge of reconsidering. Eleni getting me ready is the equivalent of a movie-style makeover. One that usually results in her tweezing a couple of random brow hairs and making me wear heels two inches above my max allowance.

But her second excited scream out the front door has me rolling my eyes and shaking my head, returning to my paused romantic comedy. It's stuck on the part where the hero makes the awkward public confession I always have to fast forward through.

I've chalked it up as being the secondhand embarrassment I felt while watching it, but maybe it's the pang of jealousy.

This morning, the news warned of a possible weather system incoming from the north. A downward spike that could bring a little bit of snow, but nothing too bad. As someone who's lived in Colorado her whole life, I know how sometimes the news can be completely wrong.

This is definitely one of those times.

My fingernails dig into the soft padding of my palm as I clench them harder around the rubber handle holding me inside the ski gondola. White flurries slap angrily against the window while the whistle of growing winds seems as loud as an oncoming train.

The storm came out of nowhere and decided to descend on me when I was thirty feet off the ground.

My heart thrums in my chest with every second as the lift

ascends up the mountain. I know I'm safe, but if the wind doesn't stop, and they have to stop the gondola... well, I can't think of a worse outcome than some rescue crew coming to get me.

For the next few minutes, I send silent pleas to Mother Nature to get me to the top. I want to take this as a sign that I should have kept my ass on my comfortable couch, but try my best to stay positive. It's hard, though, when my body's swaying with every gust and the chains above are singing their sweet melody of tension. I'm not necessarily terrified of heights, but I'm also not very comfortable with them either.

Almost there. Almost there.

I repeat it over and over until finally, the light of the resort shines through the storm, relieving some of my heart's palpitations. When the lift finally stops and the attendant opens my door, I all but jump out, nearly running into him.

"I'm sorry," I tell him, gripping the side rail.

He shakes his head. "Not a problem. We're actually about to close this until the storm passes."

I start to nod my understanding, but then something concerning grabs hold of my esophagus. "How long until that happens? I'm not an overnight guest."

Going on a first date isn't too bad. Doing it on Valentine's is a little rough. But being stuck at the restaurant? I'd rather stand on stage and sing karaoke. Which is saying a lot.

The attendant shrugs. "They say it should pass within the hour."

Relief slinks through me, only to disappear. The news said we wouldn't be getting slammed with a storm at all, either.

Shit.

Before I follow the path up to the resort, I text my sister about how I've narrowly escaped the icy jaws of death and how she better fly a hot-air balloon to pick me up later if the lifts stay closed. Luckily, though, this is probably the best place to get stranded.

Cupid's Peak is one of the nicest ski resorts in the state. It's been featured on multiple forums since its opening as number one, and I can attest to the absolute beauty of it.

Eleni and I were sent here as part of our company retreat, and honestly, it's secretly one of the reasons I agreed to the date.

It's as beautiful as I remember. Three stories of floor-to-ceiling glass windows line the front, while twelve floors of immaculate rooms twist around in the shape of a C. Each room comes with a massive balcony, some of which even have hot tubs and fireplaces, while all of them look more like large studio apartments than hotel rooms.

The restaurant is equally impressive, and my stomach growls at the memory of the roasted rack of lamb.

Inside the lobby, warmth envelops me, wrapping around my body like a warm towel after a shower. A shiver runs through me nonetheless as I approach the large oak desk.

The host greets me, her bright red lips curling with a genuine smile. "Good afternoon. So glad you made it safely. Are you checking in?"

I shake my head. "I'm here for a dinner reservation. Last name is de la Cruz."

The woman nods before typing something on the computer. Her eyes search the screen briefly before they widen. "Oh. You're here for—"

She snaps her attention to someone behind me, making me jolt. A gentleman appears from seemingly nowhere and holds out a hand. "May I take your coat?"

My gaze bounces back between the host and him. "Uh, sure." I strip the jacket from my arms and hand it to him. The host's eyes drop the length of my body, and for a moment, a wave of appreciation for my sister's work washes over me. "What were you saying before?"

As the man hands me a coat ticket, a tiny warning in the back of my head is starting to sound. Suddenly, I'm a hell of a lot more nervous than I was a moment ago.

The host shakes her head and comes from around the counter. "I'll lead you through now. We moved your table to the booths near the back. It's more private and out of direct view of most of the dining area. More romantic, if you will."

My brows squeeze together. "I'm sorry. I'm a little confused. Why did you need to move us?"

The host gives me another smile, but this one is a little more along the lines of "isn't it obvious" before leading me into the attached restaurant. The lights are much dimmer than I remember, and every single table is full. There're couples everywhere, most of which are casually eating, while a few others seem as though they're two seconds away from wanting to suck each other's faces off.

My stomach twists as she takes me around to a row of booths next to the tall glass windows overlooking the slopes. It's an incredible view of the current storm, but it's also extremely intimate and not really meant for a first date. Especially not a blind one.

"Excuse me," I try again. "Can you please tell me—"

"Here we are." The host stops abruptly at the last small U-shaped booth, where a man sits with his back to me. "I'll have your server right over."

I don't even get to thank her before she disappears, but then again, I probably wouldn't be able to. Not when the man has turned around and crushed gray eyes collide with mine.

You've got to be fucking kidding me.

"Hey, Mia. It's been a while."

Acknowledgments

Thank you, my reader, for filling your time with the stories in my head.

As always, thank you to my hubs who made this book possible with wrangling the kids and cooking me yummy meals. To my kids for always walking in when I'm writing the spiciest scenes. And to my incredible alphas and betas.

M.L., Dominque, Lily, Alexa, Salma, Skarlet, Erica, Lo, Batool Zainab, and Andrea.

Y'all are the effing bomb and I hope you never leave me! Thank you for putting up with me being so last minute and needing everything done in one day. Like seriously. I love y'all.

CATTTTT. You came through. I can't thank you enough for creating such an incredible cover and blowing me away with your talent yet again. I'm so incredibly lucky to have you.

Again, thank you to everyone! I can't wait for the next holiday I randomly decide to pop one of these bad boys out! Stay tuned.

About the Author

Lee Jacquot is a wild-haired bibliophile who writes romances with strong heroines that deserve a happy ever after. When Lee isn't writing or drowning herself in a good book, she laughs or yells at one of her husband's practical jokes.

Lee is addicted to cozy pajamas, family games nights, and making tents with her kids. She currently lives in Texas with her husband, and three littles. She lives off coffee and Dean Winchester.

Visit her on Instagram or TikTok to find out about upcoming releases and other fun things! @authorleejacquot